"Before we go eat there's
I need to do. Something I believe we
both need me to do."

His fingers went into her hair, caressed her nape, giving her time to protest should she so desire—because she knew what he was about to do. Eli was going to kiss her. Her heart pounded against her ribcage, threatening to burst free. The man she had dreamed of kissing her so many times was actually going to put his mouth against hers of his own free will. Miracles happened every day.

He felt amazing.

Better than anything she'd ever imagined— and she'd imagined lots.

Her heels not giving her the steadiness she needed to keep from ending up an ooey-gooey puddle in the floor, she leaned into him…aligned her body _just so_ against his. Her arms wrapped around him, touching, putting every sinew into her memory, every ripple of his muscles, the texture of his skin, the intense heat radiating from his every pore.

She savored the feel of him, the smell, the taste, the intensity of him. This was Eli.

She was _kissing_ Eli.

Dear Reader

Some time back I reconnected with a friend who met a man online, fell in love with him before she'd ever met him in person, and is now happily married to him with two kids. Since then I've been thinking about how technology has changed the way people find each other in this crazy, busy world we live in, and how individual love stories begin in so many ways. My friend met her man online, felt a spark, and quickly began texting that led to sexting, and their in-person relationship developed from there. The sexting someone you'd never met intrigued me, because of the trust that would have to be involved before I'd ever risk doing that.

Much like myself, Nurse Beth Taylor can't imagine ever sexting or sending risqué photographs of herself. Actually, she can't even imagine anyone in her life who would send her a sext. So when she gets a late-night photo of some washboard abs she's convinced it's her best friend pulling a prank on her. How is she to know when she texts back that she's actually texting her fantasy guy?

If Dr Eli Randolph's ex-girlfriend was as perfect for him as everyone kept telling him, why wasn't he able to take that last step with her? *He* had to be the problem. Only when he sends an accidental text never meant to be sent—and to the wrong woman at that—he finds himself quickly caught up in an excitement he hasn't felt in for ever. Texting isn't enough. Eli wants the real thing. Only how does he recover a relationship that started with a text meant for another woman?

I hope you enjoy Eli and Beth's story as much as I enjoyed writing it. Drop me an email at Janice@janicelynn.net to share your thoughts about their romance, about how our cyber world has changed romance, or just to say hello.

Happy reading!

Janice

FLIRTING WITH THE DOC OF HER DREAMS

BY
JANICE LYNN

Published in Great Britain 2014
by Mills & Boon, an imprint of Harlequin (UK) Limited,
Large Print edition 2015
Eton House, 18-24 Paradise Road,
Richmond, Surrey, TW9 1SR

© 2014 Janice Lynn

ISBN: 978-0-263-25463-1

Harlequin (UK) Limited's policy is to use papers that are natural, renewable and recyclable products and made from wood grown in sustainable forests. The logging and manufacturing processes conform to the legal environmental regulations of the country of origin.

Printed and bound in Great Britain
by CPI Antony Rowe, Chippenham, Wiltshire

Janice Lynn has a Masters in Nursing from Vanderbilt University, and works as a nurse practitioner in a family practice. She lives in the southern United States with her husband, their four children, their Jack Russell—appropriately named Trouble—and a lot of unnamed dust bunnies that have moved in since she started her writing career.

To find out more about Janice and her writing visit www.janicelynn.com

Recent titles by Janice Lynn:

THE ER'S NEWEST DAD
NYC ANGELS: HEIRESS'S BABY SCANDAL*
CHALLENGING THE NURSE'S RULES
FLIRTING WITH THE SOCIETY DOCTOR
DOCTOR'S DAMSEL IN DISTRESS
THE NURSE WHO SAVED CHRISTMAS
OFFICER, SURGEON…GENTLEMAN!
DR DI ANGELO'S BABY BOMBSHELL
PLAYBOY SURGEON, TOP-NOTCH DAD

NYC Angels

Janice won
The National Readers' Choice Award
for her first book
THE DOCTOR'S PREGNANCY BOMBSHELL

Dedication

To Michael. Thanks for making me believe in
happily ever after when I'd forgotten how.
I love you.

CHAPTER ONE

ROLLING OVER IN bed and grabbing her cellular phone off the nightstand, sleepy-eyed nurse Beth Taylor squinted at the lit screen.

Who'd be texting her at…? She registered the time at just before midnight and winced. She'd just pulled two twelve-hour ICU shifts that had each been more along the line of sixteen hours. Exhausted, she'd hit the sack minutes after getting home.

The last thing she'd been expecting had been to be awakened by a text message. The phone number wasn't one she recognized. If this was some sales advertisement she was going to scream.

Fighting a yawn, and her vision blurred with sleep, she touched the screen, opening the message.

Hello. If that was for sale, sign her up.

All traces of sleep vanishing, she stared at the text. More aptly at the photo burning her screen.

Burning her eyes into flaming orbs.

Wow.

She glanced at the number again and racked her brain, trying to figure out who the number belonged to.

Not one she knew.

Neither were those abs any she'd ever had the pleasure of setting eyes on in person. Ha, not even close. She only wished some hot guy would send her a picture like that. Sadly, hot or not, this was the closest she'd gotten to a bare male body outside the hospital—and that so didn't count—since her break-up with Barry almost a year ago.

Okay, so the truth was she didn't want some random hot guy to sext her, neither did she want her ex to sext her, text her, or anything else. It was one scorching hot man in particular she wanted paying her attention. Unfortunately, he already had an equally hot girlfriend and didn't know Beth existed. Still, Dr. Eli Randolph was her fantasy guy, had been from the first time she'd seen him smile the day she'd started at Cravenwood Hospital a few months ago.

She wasn't quite sure what it was about him that had hooked her so intently. Yes, he was total eye candy, but it was something beyond his looks, something deeper, something about the glimmer in his eyes, the sincerity in his laugh, the kindness with which he dealt with his patients and coworkers, and, yes, the warmth of his smile. She really liked the man's smile. Then there was the outer packaging to all that inner wonderfulness that just made her knees weak. Eli was the whole package.

He was also someone else's.

She would never step across that boundary. She'd been on the opposite side of that coin and it wasn't a fun place to be. Never would she do that to someone.

Still, a girl was allowed a secret fantasy or two, right? Especially when that girl was as beat as she currently was. Perhaps she was so tired she was hallucinating the entire sext thing.

Maybe one of her friends was playing a joke on her.

A light bulb went off in her head. Sighing, she looked at the photo again. Yeah, that was a very realistic scenario now that she thought of it.

She'd pulled a prank on Emily earlier that week and her best friend had promised retribution. Hadn't Emily mentioned a new phone application a while back where one could have their number appear as someone else's?

Better to just ignore Emily than to encourage her. No telling what her roommate from college would do if given a little slack. Beth had learned that long before she'd moved to be near her friend when she'd wanted to make a fresh start far away from Barry and his new fiancée.

Stop sexting me, you perv.

Beth set her phone back on her night stand, punched her pillow, and prayed those sexted abs made an appearance in her dreams. At least in her dreams she should have a fabulous sex life, right?

At any rate, Emily couldn't accuse her of showing how desperate she actually was. Her life, particularly her love life, was boring, boring, boring. Her best friend knew that and kept encouraging her to quit letting a man who didn't know she existed hold up her love life. Problem was, no real-life man measured up to her fantasy guy.

Emily also frequently voiced that Beth might have subconsciously become fascinated by someone out of her reach so she didn't have to move on beyond what had happened with Barry so she wouldn't get hurt again. Wrong. She was so over that jerk who'd screwed her over. She knew not all men went back to their old girlfriends. Anyone who met Dr. Eli Randolph would know exactly why she'd become fascinated by him. It didn't have a thing to do with her old hang-ups. The man was mega-hot and brilliant to boot.

Still, she really should take Emily's advice and get a life outside work. Maybe she would go out with that guy from Administration who'd asked her to dinner a few times. She closed her eyes, saw a flash of blue eyes, curly brown hair, and a smile that took her breath away—all of which did not belong to the admin guy, but instead to a certain fantasy doctor.

Now wide awake, she rolled over in bed, picked up her phone and decided she might as well tell her friend she was onto her.

Leaning back against the leather sofa he'd sunk onto, Dr. Eli Randolph wondered just how low he'd gone.

Grimacing, he stared at the reply to his idiotic accidental text message.

Obviously not as low as he was going to go.

He raked his fingers over his tired eyes and shook his head in frustration.

He should have known better than to have taken that picture, much less considered sending it to his ex-girlfriend…or whomever he'd sent the bare-bellied photo to.

He'd been erasing Cassidy's phone number one digit at a time, retyping it, time and again, wondering what was wrong with him that he couldn't be happy with such an ideal-for-him woman, that her unexpected sext message and photo hadn't provoked any of the right feelings inside him when logically it should have. She was a beautiful woman. What was wrong with him? Berating himself for not being able to love her the way he should, he'd hit a random number, realized what he'd done and gone to erase it, but had accidentally hit send instead.

He'd sent an inappropriate photo to a complete stranger whose phone number was one number off his perfect ex-girlfriend's.

Perfect.

There went that word again. Tonight the word nauseated him.

Everyone was always telling him how lucky he was, how he had the perfect girlfriend, how he and Cassidy were the perfect couple, how he had the perfect life. Perfect. Perfect Cassidy. He'd dumped her a couple of weeks ago because of…he didn't know why, just that he had told her they should start seeing other people.

Truth was Cassidy was the perfect woman. He'd spent three years of his life with her and had imagined he'd grow old with the pretty blonde hospitalist. Yet recently, when she'd started hinting about a ring, questioning why they hadn't taken that next step, something had held him back. For lack of a better explanation, he'd told her they lacked physical passion. Tonight, she'd sexted him in ways that should put physical passion into any relationship. He'd wanted to feel something, but hadn't. Knowing the problem lay within him and not within perfect Cassidy, he'd toyed with the idea of sexting back, to try to make himself feel something, anything. What was the worst thing that could happen?

He frowned at his cellular phone. What indeed?

Never in his life had he snapped pictures of his own body. But, nevertheless, he'd raised his shirt, flexed his abdominal muscles, snapped a picture, and let the thing sit unsent on his phone for over an hour. The sickening feeling in his belly had held him back, just as the feeling had held him back from giving in to Cassidy's desire that he propose. No amount of sexting or wishing was going to make him want to marry Cassidy.

There was something wrong with him that he wanted more than a perfect woman, that he couldn't be content with the idea of Cassidy as his wife and the mother of his children, that he couldn't see himself waking up next to her for the next fifty-plus years. He hadn't lied when he'd told her they lacked physical passion. He just didn't feel a spark. Hadn't in so long he couldn't recall if there ever had been a spark or if she'd so ideally matched his criteria of what he wanted in a woman that he'd just imagined electricity between them.

Thank God he'd had enough sense to only snap his midsection. No face and nothing below the waist. The worst thing that could happen was he could be reported for harassment and his picture could be a social media blunder sensation, right?

His phone buzzed again. Wincing, he opened the text that no doubt would blast him for his depravity. Deservedly so. Maybe he should just apologize and admit to having sent the message by accident.

By the way, I know this is you, Emily. What did you do? Download that application to make your number appear as someone else's? I'm so onto you. No worries. You didn't interrupt anything in this girl's bedroom except sleep.

Whoever had gotten his text thought he was someone else. That was fortunate. He should let it go at that, not say or do anything more. So why was he texting back? Boredom? Curiosity? Insanity?

What would you like me to have interrupted?

Feeling an even bigger fool than when he'd realized he'd sent the message and to the wrong number, he wondered at the force within him that had directed his fingers to reply. He really was messed up in the head, perhaps just from fatigue, but he definitely wasn't thinking straight. He closed his eyes and waited for about thirty seconds before his phone buzzed.

Ha. As if you don't already know the answer to that.

Remind me.

Dr. Eli Randolph tied to my bed and at the mercy of my tongue.

Eli's jaw dropped. His brows rose. He stared at the number. He wasn't tired any more. He was curious. Who had he sexted? Why was he typing out another message, because this had to be some kind of joke.

What would you do to Dr. Randolph with your tongue?

He'd started typing "me" and had to change it to "Dr. Randolph."

The same thing every other living breathing woman wants to do to that man with her tongue.

Eli doubted that most women would even give him the time of day much less have tongue fantasies about him, especially if they knew there was something wrong with him emotionally. Okay, so he was a decent guy—minus the wayward random sext message and lack of ability to take that final step in a relationship—he enjoyed exercise and sports to where he stayed in decent shape, worked hard to where he had financial security, and he lived a good life. All of which had inspired Cassidy to want to shop for rings, but no tongue fantasies for either of them. Lord, how long had it been since he'd even let his mind fantasize about a woman? Any woman? To just close his eyes and think about sex?

With Cassidy, he'd thought about how compatible they were, how well they got along, how they could have the perfect life together, how she'd pass along her good genes to his children, but he hadn't been able to take the steps that would bring all those things to fruition. Just as he hadn't thought about sex.

He was a man. He should have been thinking about sex at least occasionally. What was wrong with him?

Tell me.

Because, crazy as it was, he wanted to know. He wanted to think about sex, to feel normal, rather than somehow lacking for not being able to commit to an amazing woman like Cassidy.

Lick every pore on his scrumptious body until he screams my name in ecstasy.

Eli swallowed. This was crazy. He was crazy. He was thinking about sex now.

What name would that be?

You're a little slow here, Em. He'd be screaming my name.

Which didn't tell him anything. He stared at his phone screen and tried to figure out how to reply. Before he could decide his phone buzzed again.

The woman he needs to dump his perfect girlfriend for and whisk me away for a wild weekend of really hot S-E-X. Our bodies slick with sweat and gliding against each other. His mouth on me. My mouth on him. That's what you should have interrupted. Not that I'd have answered your text had I been doing any of those things.

Eli gulped. He was not a guy who got off on this kind of thing. He was sure of it.

Dr. Randolph doesn't have a girlfriend, he typed. They were no longer a couple even if she had sent him the unexpected sext message. He'd thought she was okay with their break-up, but maybe he'd been wrong. Regardless, he wouldn't be changing his mind. That he couldn't respond to her sext message, that he had sent his fumbled attempt to a stranger, that he was more stimulated by a text conversation with that stranger than his ex-girlfriend spoke volumes.

Which was crazy. For all he knew, he could be texting with an eighty-year-old granny. Or a man.

Now, there was a buzz killer of a thought.

No, the texter had implied she was female when she'd said it was the same thing every woman wanted and when she'd said "this girl's bedroom." He was texting with a female. A female around his age. He was sure of it.

Dr. Randolph and Dr. Qualls broke up? When? Why haven't you told me this? What kind of best friend are you?

He should put his phone down and not text any more. He wasn't a man who texted with women he didn't know. Totally not cool and not his style. He'd broken things off with his perfect girlfriend and needed to figure out what was wrong with him, not become some weirdo who texted with strangers.

Or not with a stranger. This was someone who knew him and Cassidy. Who?

A couple of weeks ago, he responded. So maybe he was a weirdo who texted with strange women.

Em, if this is your idea of a joke, I'm going to kill you.

Why would this Em person joke about him and Cassidy having broken up?

Are you sure? I hadn't heard that and you know how everyone at the hospital gossips.

He doubted many people knew about them having broken up. Not that he cared who knew, but he hadn't advertised the fact around the hospital. His private life wasn't his coworkers' business. He doubted Cassidy had told many people either.

Positive.

They'd stay broken up. He'd truly believed Cassidy to be the woman he'd spend his life with. Maybe he just hadn't been ready for marriage; maybe when the time was right, his expectations wouldn't be so impossible. Maybe.

They're still friends.

Picture me rolling my eyes, Em. She was clearly in love with him. If they're still friendly it's because she hopes they'll get back together.

Was that why she'd sexted him tonight? Because she'd hoped to spark physical passion and for them to get back together? Deep down, Eli knew the reasons he hadn't proposed to Cassidy went much deeper than their lack of physical passion. Something more than sex had been missing. Which was why he knew there was a problem with him. Cassidy was his best friend, a beautiful woman, brilliant, good-hearted, and he'd broken up with her because when it came to the rest of his life, he wanted more. He was insane.

Was it also insane that he wished he could picture the texter rolling her eyes? That he'd like some visual image to go with their conversation? He had friends who'd dated via meeting someone on social media. He'd thought them nuts, but maybe there was something to the anonymity of it all that let a person step outside their normal shells. Certainly, he'd never imagined himself being intrigued by a stranger saying she wanted to tie him to a bed and lick him. But he was.

If she's smart she'll win him back.

Eli shook his head at his phone. Not going to happen. Ever. Until tonight he honestly hadn't thought Cassidy wanted to win him back. She'd accepted his ending things as if she'd already come to the same conclusion.

How would you win him back?

Hell-o! I'd never have lost him to begin with, came the immediate response.

Eli laughed, liking the texter's spunk. Yeah, he wished he had a visual to go with the messages.

I'd have him tied to my bed and at my mercy, remember?

How could I forget?

Eli closed his eyes and tried to imagine being tied to a bed. He'd never done that. Never given up control during sex, or to a woman, not that there had been that many. There hadn't.

I guess you have heard me mention my obsession with Dr. Randolph a time or two, huh, Em? Sorry.

Obsession? With him? Who was he texting with? Was it someone who had recognized his number and was having fun at his expense?

Em. Emily. He racked his brain. The only Emilys he knew were Emily Jacobs, a bright dyed red-haired registered nurse who worked in the hospital emergency department most of the time, but occasionally filled in at ICU, and the Emily from high school who had sat behind him in chemistry, but he hadn't seen her in years. Then again, Craven-wood was a decent-sized college town. There were probably hundreds of Emilys in the middle Tennessee area. But this one was privy to hospital gossip. Were there other Emilys at Cravenwood Hospital?

Game's up, Em. You've had your fun. We both know the perfect couple are still in hotness bliss.

Eli winced at the texter's use of the word perfect.
Maybe you're right and I just need to forget him, the texter continued, and Eli felt her frustration in each word.

I can't believe you chose tonight to do this. You know I just pulled two sixteen-hour shifts thanks to Leah being out sick.

Leah being out sick. Whoever this was definitely worked at the hospital with him. Bells rang in Eli's head.

Leah Windham?

She's the only Leah in ICU. You've had your fun. We've both got to be at the hospital early in the morning. Go kiss your hunky boyfriend and let me sleep. Goodnight, Emily.

Goodnight.

Whoever she was.

"This isn't funny," Beth insisted, grabbing an apple from the lunch line and wishing she could squeeze it like a stress ball. "'Fess up. You were just telling me about that phone app that makes your number appear as someone else's last week. I know it was you last night."

Following closely behind her in the hospital cafeteria lunch line, her best friend snickered. "I wish it had been, but I'm telling you, it wasn't me."

Emily had insisted the same thing earlier in the day when she had called the ICU regarding a patient and Beth had asked about the messages. She still wasn't convinced her friend hadn't sent the texts. The body build was wrong for the photo to have been a posed shot of Eddie, but Emily could have easily found the picture online. It was just the kind of thing jokester Emily would do. No doubt her friend would play the prank out a bit longer.

"You should show me the text messages," Emily said as they sat down at a table in the hospital cafeteria. Not that either of them would be able to stay there long. Beth was surprised her friend had been able to sneak away from the emergency department at all. As a nurse, one never knew if you'd actually get a lunch break or not.

"You should confess that you sent the messages."

Emily shook her head. "Wasn't me, I promise." Her friend waggled her perfectly waxed brows and crossed her heart. "Hope you didn't say anything incriminating."

"You know exactly what I said and about whom."

Her friend's eyes widened. "You revealed your crush on Dr. Randolph—" her friend mouthed the name rather than speaking it out loud in case someone t overheard "—to the mystery texter? As in, you gave a name?"

The absolute shock on Emily's heart-shaped face had Beth's stomach spasming. Despite the local theater her friend often volunteered at she wasn't that good an actress, was she?

Trying to pretend she wasn't freaking out inside, Beth took a bite of her apple, chewed slowly, let loose an inner scream of denial, then shrugged. "I don't want to discuss this any more."

"I do." Emily's eyes glowed with excitement. "I want to know who you were texting with, because Eddie seriously had me otherwise occupied last night."

Trying to squash her doubts and thoughts of what her best friend claimed to have been doing instead, Beth shrugged. "Then I guess we'll never know, will we?"

Lord, she hoped her friend was teasing, that Emily had been the texter, as she'd been so positive about the night before when she'd been too tired to think clearly. Good ole Emily. Always pulling her leg and trying to push her out of her comfortable protective shell.

"Sure we will."

Beth cut her gaze to her best friend. "How?"

"Hello." Emily snapped her fingers in front of Beth's face. "You're smarter than that."

Realization dawned and Beth's jaw dropped. "Uh-uh. No way am I calling that number."

Emily held out her hand. "Fine. I will. Give me your phone."

"No way." Beth's gut clenched into tight knots. "If I wasn't texting with you, then I prefer not knowing who now knows my biggest secret. How humiliating?!"

Emily didn't look impressed by Beth's inner misery. "So what if someone knows you think Dr. Randolph is the cat's meow? The man is hot. It's a fact."

Beth couldn't stop her blush.

"Plus, if what you said is true and he and Dr. Qualls have broken up, then he's fair game now." Emily waggled her perfectly plucked brows. "If you ask me, you should tell him you think he's one fine specimen of a man."

Beth went into sensory overload and mental shutdown any time the man was near. The last thing she should do was tell him how fine she thought he was. She shook her head. "I don't know that they've broken up. Plus, even if they have broken up, they'll probably just get back together."

"Ask him, and you can't judge every man by what Barry did."

Beth shook her head harder, faster, as if that made her response more negative and would jar Barry Neal from her mind forever.

"You have a serious problem, you know."

Beth knew.

"You let a stupid ex influence how you view all men, influence how you dress and act, and then, when you finally start getting over him, you fall crazy in lust with a man you avoid at all costs. I've never seen feet move as fast as yours any time he comes near." Emily gave a disappointed sigh. "I really think this whole Eli thing is just another way for you to avoid getting back into the dating saddle."

"Maybe." But she really didn't think so because she'd like to be back in the dating saddle. As far as the way she dressed and acted went, Emily was referring to her college days. One couldn't wear streaks of blue in one's hair, a nose ring, and colorful Hello Kitty T-shirts and retro make-up forever. The changes in her had nothing to do with Barry having crushed her heart and spirit. She'd grown up, had a more mature look, that was all.

"You're crazy," Emily accused.

If she'd revealed her silly schoolgirl crush on Dr. Randolph to some stranger then she couldn't argue with her friend's assessment of her mental state. She was crazy.

Crazy about a man who didn't know she existed.

Whether to distract himself of his failure with Cassidy or for some other insane reason, Eli had thought of little other than the previous night's text messages. He'd even gone so far as to try to track down who the number belonged to via the internet but had been unsuccessful as the number wasn't a public one.

He couldn't seem to put the messages from his head.

Especially at moments like the present one.

Moments he was at the hospital and searching every face as if somehow he'd figure out who the texter was by the look on her face. What did he expect? That the truth would be stamped across her forehead like a scarlet letter?

Most likely, whoever the texter was, she worked in ICU since she'd had to work late to cover for Leah Windham. She was also probably a nurse. Which made sense since she was friends with Emily Jacobs.

With a little patience and a leading conversation to find out who'd worked late the night before, he'd have this figured out before the day ended.

Usually he rivaled Job on the patience score, but today he just felt antsy. He wanted to know whom he'd been texting. Why it was so imperative, he wasn't sure—he just needed to know.

He'd actually considered asking Emily which one of her friends was obsessed with him, but figured the woman would tell him where he could go rather than give him a name.

"Dr. Randolph?" A pleasant female in her mid-fifties caught him just as he'd been heading for the elevator. "A patient is being admitted to 303 with a pulmonary embolism and you've been consulted on her," the charge nurse told him. "She's not on the floor yet, but should be within a half hour."

"Thanks, Ruth." Glancing at his watch, he figured he should grab something to eat while still at the hospital. Then hopefully the new admission would be on the floor and he'd do the consult prior to heading back to his office to start his afternoon appointments.

Maybe, just maybe, while in the ICU, he'd get a glimpse of whoever he'd been texting with the night before, because, whoever she was, his interest was piqued.

CHAPTER TWO

"DON'T LOOK NOW, but guess who just walked into the cafeteria."

Before her friend had said a word, Beth knew exactly who had walked into the cafeteria where she and Emily were eating their lunch. Her Dr. Eli Randolph radar had started bleeping. Big time. Bleep. Bleep. Bleep. Which sounded ridiculous but all her senses seemed to be tuned into the man. Whenever he came around, she was just…bleeping aware.

Which made her palms sweat, her tongue thick, and her feet antsy.

Which had led to her asking her superior to please avoid assigning her to Dr. Randolph's patients. Nurse Rogers might have thought her request odd, but without too many questions and an empathetic look she'd said she would do her best. She couldn't avoid doing so altogether, of course, but for the most part she had attempted to accommodate Beth's request and the few times she'd had to, Beth had avoided him during rounds.

"What if he is single now?" Emily asked, not willing to let go of their subject. "What are you going to do about him?"

Beth grimaced. "I never should have told you that I find him attractive."

"You more than find him attractive. I've known you since college, have seen you through your two major relationships, and knew you way before Barry messed up your head and your sense of style. I would have known."

Ugh at the reminder of her ex. She couldn't care less about Barry, but her stupidity still stung. She could point out that it wasn't her head Barry had messed up. It had been her heart, but what was one organ compared to another? Either way, she'd gotten over the cheater the hard way.

"I see how you look at that man so it's not as if you could hide how you feel from me," Emily pointed out, her gaze raking over Eli as if sizing him up. "I could point out that you never lit up like this around the doofus who left you for his ex and that Barry wasn't even fit to tie Eli's dirty ole tennis shoes."

No, she hadn't lit up around Barry. Just as well as he'd done the un-decent thing of sleeping with his ex while still living with Beth. Men.

"My question is, are you going to act on that attraction? Tell him you think he's hot?"

Emily's question snapped Beth back to the present and she frowned at her friend.

"Don't be ridiculous and quit staring at him," she ordered, but was unable to stop herself from doing the same. What was it about Eli that got to her so? Besides the fact that he was brilliant, breathtaking, and had the most amazing smile of any man ever, that was. "I've worked with him for months, and I seriously doubt he even knows my name. Why would I make a fool of myself that way?"

Why indeed?

"Because if you don't, some other smarter, braver woman will and then you'll still be pining after him from afar while he becomes someone else's boyfriend because you were too chicken to go after the man of your dreams."

Ouch. Emily didn't mince her words.

"From afar is good." At least from afar she could still breathe. But Eli with another woman…okay, so that thought made every organ in her body twist up like a wrung dishrag. Still, it wasn't as if she wasn't used to him having a girlfriend. He had from the moment she'd met him and felt whatever that instant crazy fluttering in her chest had been. Not that he'd felt it. He hadn't. Not that he'd noticed. He hadn't. So why should the fact that he might no longer have a girlfriend matter? She obviously hadn't made an impression.

Plus she'd had a relationship with a man who'd had a perfect ex and ultimately he'd gone back to the woman he'd invested so much time in. No thanks on a heartbreak repeat.

"From afar sucks," Emily needlessly pointed out. "Admit it."

Okay, she admitted it. To herself at any rate. Emily was right. From afar did suck. Not making an impression on a man you couldn't quit thinking about sucked. Being told that dating you had made your ex realize his ex hadn't really been that bad after all? That sucked a big one too.

"If you don't at least let him know that you're interested, I'll know that you really are using him as a shield from jumping back into the dating world."

"That's not what I'm doing. The man is wonderful. You've admitted as much yourself."

"True, so prove it."

Prove it? What did her friend want her to do? March up and tell him she wanted to lick him from head to toe? That she thought about him way too much morning, noon, and night?

"Look." Her stomach clenching into a tight knot, Beth gestured toward where Eli stood. He wasn't alone. A gorgeous blonde bombshell with kind blue eyes and an almost always present smile had joined him. "Dr. Qualls is smiling at him like crazy." And touching his arm quite possessively. Ugh. Not that Beth had any right to feel the green flowing through her veins.

She'd already resigned herself that Eli and Cassidy would marry and for the rest of her life she'd watch them from afar, wondering, What if? Emily was right. From afar did suck, but there were some things that were just wrong. Going after another woman's man was one of them, especially when that woman was someone as nice as Dr. Qualls. At least she hadn't liked Barry's ex. Not that she'd known her well, but Cassidy Qualls seemed to be a class act inside and out. "I don't think they've broken up."

Eyeing the couple, Emily waved her fork. "Actually, I think your sexter was right. I think they have. Look."

Beth forced her gaze back toward the couple. Dr. Qualls still stood there, but she was no longer smiling. A pensive, unsure expression on her lovely face, she was watching Eli walk away and sit down at a table. By himself.

Oh, wow. Could he possibly be single? She hadn't dared dream it possible. Well, she had dared, but hadn't believed that her weird texter could have been right.

"I think you should go and talk to him."

What? The man's girlfriend—ex-girlfriend?—was standing ten feet from him. His nice ex-girlfriend whom Beth admired and thought a great hospitalist and often thought that if she had to pick someone to be like, she'd pick Cassidy Qualls. The woman had it all. But had she perhaps lost the one thing Beth envied her?

"No way. What would I say?" She took a drink, her gaze darting back and forth between Eli and Cassidy, looking for a clue to the truth. They weren't behaving normally, that was for sure. Probably a lovers' spat that they'd soon recover from.

"Hello." Emily mimicked Beth's voice and mannerisms. "My name is Beth Taylor and I want to have your children."

Water spewed from Beth's mouth and she gasped at her best friend. "I do not!"

"Sure you do but, okay, let me try again," Emily cleared her throat and started over, still doing a fairly decent impression of Beth's voice. "My name is Beth Taylor. I'd like to rip your clothes off with my teeth and have you for breakfast, lunch, and dinner on a regular basis." Emily fluttered her eyelashes. "Be forewarned, I'm a girl with a hearty appetite."

True, but not words Beth could see spilling from her mouth during a conversation with him. Words in general had difficulty spilling from her mouth when she spoke to Eli, which was yet another reason why she avoided him.

She glanced toward where he sat alone at a rectangular table for six. He had on blue scrubs that were a little darker than the shade of his eyes. His slightly curly brown hair was rumpled, as if he'd run his fingers through it more often than usual today. Another doctor, a cardiologist, came over and must have asked if he could join him. Nodding, Eli smiled at the man and Beth's heart thump-thump-thumped.

Crazy how something as simple as his smile caused her body to react so profoundly. She'd probably go into cardiac arrest and need the services of that cardiologist if Eli ever aimed one of those smiles directly at her. That would be her luck. He'd walk by, smile politely, and she'd fall over. Kaput. At least she'd die knowing that if he was that close he'd perform mouth to mouth and that would be the last thing she felt against her lips. Hmm, might be worth meeting her maker a little sooner.

"I see you aren't denying that one," Emily pointed out with an all-too-smug grin.

Her friend was right. She wanted to gobble Eli up and go back for seconds. And thirds. And… Beth sighed. "At least that diet sounds like one I could stick to," she conceded with a slight shrug.

Emily laughed. "Regardless of your reasons for being interested in Dr. Randolph, if he's single you really should let him know you're interested. Not every man is Barry, whom I personally never thought good enough for you anyway, nor did he ever rev your juices the way Dr. Randolph does."

No one had ever affected her the way Eli did. Just

thinking about him made her heart pound and her body clench with excited flutters. If by some grace of God they did date, but then Eli told her that dating her made him realize how wonderful Cassidy was, at least she would understand that. The woman was the total package—looks, brains, heart.

"Dr. Randolph is a good man," Emily continued between waves of her fork. "A hot man. You'll regret it always if you don't at least try. Go for it."

"That doesn't mean Dr. Randolph would be interested in me." His tastes obviously ran to quite the opposite of her. Tall, blonde, perfect.

"Why wouldn't he be? You're smart, pretty, fun, kind, a little quirky at times, but, hey, no one is perfect...except me." Emily grinned.

"That's a given." She half smiled at her friend's exception and didn't point out that she'd just labeled Cassidy as perfect as well.

"You know you want him."

From the moment she'd first seen him. Never had she felt such a crazy intense attraction. Not for any of her few high-school and college boyfriends, or for Barry, whom she'd thought she'd marry. Emily was right. From the beginning there had been something different about Eli and quite frankly that terrified her.

"As I've pointed out, that doesn't mean he'd want me in return. He's never even noticed me."

Emily failed to look impressed by Beth's argument. "I'm not quite sure how he could have since you go into hibernation any time he comes onto the ICU floor, but hello!" Emily snapped her fingers in front of Beth's face. "The man has had a girlfriend. One he has been in a relationship with for a long time. He's a good guy, not one who has a wandering eye while in a relationship. It's a good quality that he hasn't noticed you up to this point. Now that he's single, you need to shake your tail feathers and make sure he does notice."

She wasn't much for shaking tail feathers these days, wouldn't even know where to start. "He may not even be single."

"He is."

"You don't know that for sure. Just because he isn't sitting with Dr. Qualls doesn't mean they've broken up. Besides, even if they have broken up, who's to say they won't get back together?"

"Wherein lies the real problem," Emily accused, then narrowed her gaze and pursed her lips. "Chicken."

Beth winced. Was she letting the past keep her from even going after what she wanted in the present? Probably. She bit the inside of her lower lip. Fantasizing about a man she considered beyond her reach had been one thing. Actually acting on that fantasy if he'd become single, well, that was another thing altogether. She'd resigned herself that Eli would never be available, that he'd always just be the man who fascinated her from afar. She'd fully expected him to marry Dr. Qualls and have beautiful children with the gifted doctor. Odds were that even if they had broken up, that's still what would happen. Beth knew the score.

But if he were single right now, at this moment…

If he was single, then what if he'd be interested in her? Even if for a short while, even if he later told her that she didn't measure up when compared to Cassidy, she wanted that shot.

Question was, what was she willing to do, to risk, to make that shot happen?

Had he been too harsh with Cassidy? Eli hoped not. He didn't want to be unkind to her. At the same time, they needed to start having more space between them. Perhaps that was wrong as last night she'd sent him sext messages and he'd briefly considered sending her one back. Much better to cut the ties for a while. She'd just claimed to have been drunk the night before, but Cassidy never drank more than a single glass of wine. Had she just been embarrassed that he'd not returned her message? If only she knew the truth.

Regardless, they were meant to be friends, not lovers. To pretend otherwise for a single second longer would be cruel to a woman he liked and respected. That was what made this all so difficult. He didn't want to lose Cassidy's friendship.

Ending their relationship had meant more than admitting there was something wrong with him that he couldn't commit to spending the rest of his life with such an amazing woman, but it also meant damaging his relationship with his best friend.

"What's up with you and Wonder Woman?" Dr. Andrew Morgan said as he joined Eli.

Eli took a deep breath, then exhaled. He preferred his personal business to be private, but he supposed it was unrealistic that his colleagues wouldn't question what had happened. "You mean Cassidy."

He supposed she was a wonder woman of sorts. There was little she couldn't do and do well. She was a great catch. He was the fool who couldn't take that next step with her because he wanted more. More of what he wasn't sure, but if Cassidy had been his soul mate surely he wouldn't have found himself backtracking when she'd hinted she wanted a ring.

"Yes, I mean Cassidy," Andrew said, as if Eli wasn't in his right mind or he'd have known exactly to whom he referred. "You two having an argument?"

He shook his head. "We decided to go our separate ways."

"She dump you?"

Eli struggled with how to answer. He didn't want to say anything that might hurt Cassidy.

"We've decided to just be friends."

"How could you possibly just be friends with a woman like Cassidy?"

Eli looked a little closer at his colleague, noting the heightened color in the man's cheeks, the rapid pulse at his throat, and the strong set to his jaw. Interesting.

"Because that's how we feel about each other.

Friendly. It's all we should have ever been." Even as he said the words out loud, the truth echoed through him.

"Sure took you long enough to figure that out."

"Tell me about it," Eli snorted, wondering why it had taken so long. "Then again, like you said, Cassidy is a wonderful woman." His family had loved her. His mother had repeatedly told him how Cassidy was everything she'd ever hoped for in a daughter-in-law. To say she'd been disappointed at his news was the understatement of the year. "A man hesitates to let her go even when he knows it isn't going to happen between them."

Andrew nodded as if he understood, but Eli could tell he obviously didn't. His mother hadn't either. For that matter, he himself didn't understand why he hadn't been content with Cassidy.

"You should ask her out." Andrew obviously felt a passion for her that Eli couldn't, no matter how much he'd wanted to.

Andrew's eyes widened, then he glanced away rapidly. "I couldn't."

"Why not? She's single. You're single. Go for it."

The man regarded him suspiciously. "You really wouldn't care?"

Eli shook his head. "I'd be happy for you if things worked out. She's a great woman and deserves a man to treat her so. I plan to date and imagine she will too. Ask her."

Andrew toyed with his fork. "Maybe I will."

It struck Eli that he should feel remorse or jealousy or some sense of loss that a woman he'd invested years with might be moving on with another man, perhaps this man. He didn't feel any of those things. Just relief that he was no longer tied to Cassidy, which again made him wonder if something was wrong with him, if he'd set his expectations so high that even a woman who was perfect for him on paper couldn't meet them.

"You should," he repeated. "A woman like her isn't likely to stay single long."

The flash of panic in Andrew's eyes said it all. He had a thing for Cassidy, but had obviously held it at bay in respect for her relationship with Eli.

That was when Emily Jacobs caught Eli's eye.

Emily Jacobs. As in the person his texter had thought he was the night before. Was the woman sitting across the cafeteria table from her his mysterious texter?

Dark hair, light colored eyes, although he couldn't

make out their exact blue-green color, creamy complexion with a spattering of freckles across her face. Naturally pretty. Somewhat familiar.

She worked in ICU. He recalled seeing her there, although usually only glimpses here and there. Odd really when he thought about it. He was in the ICU a lot. How come his path rarely crossed this woman's—Beth something—in the ICU?

Unless she purposely avoided him.

Why would she do that?

Unless she was the texter and because of her attraction to him she'd purposely steered clear.

It was a possibility. One he wanted to put to the test.

"Excuse me," he said to the man lost in his thoughts sitting across from him, and pulled out his cellular phone. He opened his text messages from the night before and glanced at the number. Was it hers? Beth's from ICU? Logic said it was, but he wanted proof, to know for sure. He hit the telephone icon button that would dial her number and watched her closely.

When she set her fork down on her plate and reached into her scrub pocket to pull out her phone, answering without looking at the number, Eli smiled.

Bingo.

His smile widened. Although he didn't quite understand, an excitement filled him that he hadn't felt in years...maybe ever.

Maybe he wasn't ready to settle down with Cassidy, maybe there was something wrong with him that was holding him back, but at the moment, he wasn't going to worry about those things. For now he was going to quit stressing about the future and his expectations, his parents' expectations, the fact he'd chosen to become single rather than marry the "perfect" woman. He was going to enjoy life, to have fun, and not take everything so seriously. Something he'd just realized that he'd forgotten to do over the past few years.

"Hello?" Beth answered, expecting to hear her nurse supervisor's voice telling her that they needed her back on the floor. Rarely did she make it through a full lunch without an interruption from a patient or one of her coworkers, which was why she usually just ate in the ICU break room. Today she'd wanted to pick Emily's brain.

Instead of Ruth telling her to come back to ICU, she heard a resounding click.

Pulling the phone away from her ear, she looked at the number.

Aiiiiggghhhhh!

"What?" Emily asked, making Beth wonder if she'd just screamed out loud or if it was the way all the blood in her body had drained that had clued her friend in that something was wrong.

"It's…" Her voice choked up.

"Come on," her friend encouraged. "Spit it out. You look like you just got news your best friend died and I know that didn't happen because I'm sitting right here."

Beth closed her eyes then held the phone out toward her friend so she could see the screen.

"What? It's clicked off. Tell me."

"It was the number."

"The number?"

"The number." She put great emphasis on her words.

"The number you thought was me?"

Wondering if one could hyperventilate to death in a hospital cafeteria, Beth nodded and struggled to get air into her vice-gripped lungs.

"What did they say?"

"Nothing."

"Nothing?" Emily looked bamfoozled.

Beth shook her head, feeling a bit bamfoozled herself. *Breathe, Beth, breathe.*

"Then why did whoever it was call you?"

She shrugged, took a deep breath, then another. "Maybe they're going to harass me."

"About what? You didn't do anything wrong."

"Nothing wrong per se, but…I might have mentioned wanting to tie up and lick a certain doctor all over."

Emily's eyes widened and then she burst out laughing. "You didn't?"

Beth grimaced at her friend's mirth and at her own foolishness. "I told you that I revealed my fascination with the man."

"That isn't the same thing as saying you want to tie up the man and for your tongue to get up close and personal with his personables."

Her friend had a point. Unfortunately.

"What else did you say?"

Beth gave a pained look. "I don't remember exactly. Something about wanting our bodies slick with sweat and gliding together."

"Oh, baby." Emily's eyes danced with delight. "I wish I had been pulling your leg and sending those messages. Sounds like some hot reading and you know I love a steamy read."

Feeling a fool, Beth nodded. "I was tired and you'd promised retribution. If I'd been thinking clearly I'd never have sent those messages."

"Like I said before, so what that you did. So what that someone knows you think Dr. Randolph's hot. What does it matter in the grand scheme of life?"

"I don't want him to find out."

"Hello." Emily snapped her fingers in front of her face again. "We've already had this conversation. You do want him to find out that you're interested in him. You need to let him know. Up close and personal." Emily waggled her brows, then added mischievously, "With your tongue. And his personables."

Fighting the panicky feeling still welling within her, Beth rolled her eyes. "You really aren't my best friend, you know. You're just some freak with great hair I tolerate because we work together."

Patting her pulled up dyed bright red locks, which matched her personality much more than any natural shade could, Emily leaned back in her chair and grinned. "You love me and we both know it."

"Sad, but true."

"Just as we both know I'm not going to let you sit on your butt while your dream man is single and needs consoling."

Beth's eyes widened. "You wouldn't."

"I would." Emily's eyes sparkled with mischief. "You make a move or Dr. Randolph and I will be having a very interesting conversation."

"You wouldn't," she repeated.

"Wanna bet on that?"

No, she didn't, because if Emily believed she was doing what was best for Beth she wouldn't hesitate to spill the beans to Eli.

Which meant that she would have to make a move herself. Otherwise there was no telling what her friend would say to him.

Taking a deep breath, she glanced toward his table. Her gaze collided with his. The air caught in her lungs and threatened to burst them.

He was looking straight at her!

He didn't look away when their eyes met.

Instead, he grinned.

Grinned.

At her.

That's when she noticed what he held in his hand.

His cellphone.

CHAPTER THREE

"HELLO, BETH."

Where was that cardiologist? Beth needed him. Pronto. Her heart was going to stop any moment. She was sure of it.

Dr. Eli Randolph was smiling at her, had just said her name.

He knew her name?

He'd said her name!

For no good reason except to speak to her. Had he ever done so before?

No. Never. She wasn't even sure that he'd ever looked directly at her before lunch today. Definitely, they'd never locked eyes. He was looking now and, try as she might for fear of what he might see, she couldn't break their eye contact.

A light shone in his twinkling blue gaze that she'd never seen before. She couldn't quite label what she saw, but she couldn't deny that a definite interest shone there.

Had whoever she'd texted with the night before revealed her secrets to Eli? Recalling his smile in the cafeteria, the phone in his hand, Beth swallowed. Had she texted with Eli the night before? Was that even possible? If so, was he toying with her because of the things she'd admitted while thinking she was talking to Emily? Or by some miracle was Eli actually interested in her? Had he intentionally texted her the night before and, dimwit that she was, she'd revealed her secret fantasies to him, not realizing who she was texting with?

Why would he have texted her? Not just texted, but sent a photo? Not really a risqué photo, but hot all the same. Nope. Her texter couldn't have been Eli. Probably the guy from Administration had snagged her cellphone number from her employee records and when she'd stuck her foot in her mouth, he'd realized he didn't stand a chance and had told Eli about her comments. A much more likely scenario.

So what was he doing now?

Tongue lassoed around her vocal cords to where speech was impossible, she blinked at him. Why was he still here? He never hung around the nurses' station, making idle chit-chat. Never that she knew of, at any rate. Until today. She'd steered clear as long as she could, checking and rechecking her patients. Each time she'd exited a room, he'd still been leaning up against the counter, making small talk with the unit secretary and two nurses standing there.

The infuriating man had hung around in the ICU as if he had nowhere else to go. Surely he had an office full of patients waiting to see him? *Why are you still here?* she'd wanted to scream. *Leave.*

But he hadn't. Instead, he smiled down at her as if he knew her every secret.

He might.

"Beth?" he prompted, when she didn't respond to his greeting.

"Drink of water," she choked out past her bound-up vocal cords by way of explanation and took off down the hallway. She could feel his eyes on her, knew her colleagues had seen the interplay between them and also watched her scurry down the hallway as if competing for a gold medal.

Eli probably thought she was weird. Her colleagues probably thought she was weird.

She *was* weird.

The man of her dreams had gone out of his way to say something to her and she'd taken flight.

Why? She'd never been a tongue-tied ninny around men, but with Eli her brain shut down. Her body, on the other hand, went into hyperdrive, every sense more acute, making her feel more aware, more alive.

Too bad she couldn't just act cool and suave around him, let him know she thought he was the cat's meow.

More like the lion's roar.

Beth crawled into her bed, exhausted from the fifteen-hour day she'd put in at the hospital yet wide awake.

No question as to why her eyes were bright and she was feeling bushy-tailed. Or as to why her brain was auditioning for the Indy 500 and gunning for pole position.

Eli.

First, in the cafeteria, smiling at her.

Then in the ICU, when he'd spoken directly to her for the first time ever.

She'd run away.

She closed her eyes and shook her head back and

forth on her pillow, disgusted at herself. What was wrong with her? She'd dated before and never been so uncool around guys.

Then again, she hadn't ever looked at any of the men she'd known and immediately wanted to get naked either. Eli Randolph made her clothes want to come off. No wonder she'd run. If she'd stuck around, she might have been arrested for indecent exposure.

Her phone buzzed on the night stand. Although not completely surprised by the noise, she jerked in her bed and grabbed for her phone.

A text.

Before she looked she knew who it would be from. The number.

But who was the person behind the number?

From the point she'd seen the phone in Eli's hand in the cafeteria, she'd asked herself, What if? What if Dr. Eli Randolph had sent her a photo because he was interested in her? He was single, had apparently been single for a couple of weeks. It was possible. Highly unlikely, but possible.

Her phone may have just buzzed with a text from Eli.

Could it be true? Her heart raced just at the remote possibility. She clutched the phone tighter in her suddenly clammy palms and read the short message.

You awake?

No, she responded, because it was the first thing that popped into her mind.

Guess you're dreaming, then.

Something like that.

I thought about you a lot today.

Shame on you.

I like that.

What?

That you make me laugh.

You should see me naked.

Had to be Eli, because there she went, trying to get rid of her clothes again.

Yes, I should.

Ha-ha. That really would make you laugh.

Doubtful, but you do make me smile. Want to know what else you make me do?

Wonder why she ran away when he said something to her? Assuming that she really was texting with Eli?

I'm all ears.

You make me really need to hear more about the things you'd do to Dr. Randolph if he were tied to your bed.

Because she was talking to Dr. Randolph? Somehow, she believed she was. The thought made her giddy happy and terrified and embarrassed all at once.

You perv.

You know you want to tell me.

Ha. That's what u think. I never should have said those things to begin with.

Why? Because you don't really want to stroke your tongue over Dr. Randolph's entire body?

Was she talking to Eli? Was he asking her outright if she wanted him? Maybe it was better that she didn't know a hundred percent. Much easier to be forthright when she might just be talking to a stranger whose path she'd never cross in real life.

I never should have told u. I thought u were someone else.

Emily?

Yes, my friend Emily.

What does your friend Emily say about you wanting to lick Dr. Randolph?

Oh, she's all for it and says I should start slurping immediately now that he's single and all. You were right on that, btw. Word spread like wildfire around the hospital this afternoon. How is it u knew he and Dr. Qualls had broken up before anyone else?

Was it because he was Dr. Randolph?

A little birdie told me.

Right. I have a little birdie in the middle of my hand that tells people who wake me up where they can go.

There you go making me laugh again.

I wasn't trying to be funny.

Which makes it all the better.

If u say so.

I do. Sorry if I woke you, but now that we've established that you are indeed awake, tell me what you're wearing.

Beth rolled her eyes at her phone.

Really? That is so cliché.

Then give me a cliché answer.

In the glow of her cellular phone Beth glanced under the bed covers at the old Nashville Predators T-shirt and the silky panties she wore. The panties were passable as sexy, maybe. The well-worn hockey T-shirt—ha, not by any stretch of the imagination.

A teddy and garters. Four-inch heels too. Customary sleepwear, you know.

Of course. Very cliché, but great visual.

Implying that he could visualize her. Of course he could visualize her. Whether it was Eli or some random guy, he'd sexted her specifically.

What are u wearing?

Who says I'm wearing anything at all.

Beth gulped. Okay, so it wasn't an image of some random guy she was picturing. Just as always, her fantasy consisted of only one man. Eli in the buff, as the owner of that magnificent abdomen and chest from the photo.

Would be a shame to cover up those abs. That picture really u?

Would it matter if it wasn't?

Depends.

On?

Your sparkly personality. That is why I'm texting with u after all.

Oh? I thought it was because you had a thing for pervs.

Beth smiled at his quick comeback.

Well, there is that.

You owe me.

I owe u nothing.

Sure you do.

What, please tell, do I owe u?

A picture.

She laughed. Not that he could hear her. But she laughed at the absolute absurdity of her sending him, whoever him was, a photo of herself. If it was Eli she was texting with, the last thing she'd want to do was scare him away with a selfie.

I wouldn't hold my breath if I was u.

If I did would you resuscitate me?

Give you a little mouth-to-mouth?

Hadn't she just that very day been thinking of Eli giving her mouth-to-mouth? If this was him, there really was some weird connection between them.

For starters

You implying it would take more than my mouth on yours to resuscitate you? Are u like old and decrepit or something? They make little blue pills for that u know.

I'm old enough to know what I want. Are you saying that your mouth on mine is all it would take to get me…resuscitated?

Ha, Beth thought, she was no siren and her experience wasn't that she drove men wild with her kisses, but this was anonymous—sort of—texting. She could say whatever she wanted. She could be a sex goddess. A sext goddess. If this was Eli for real, well, at least while texting from the privacy of her own bed she wasn't tongue-tied, breathless, or running away from him. She kind of liked the freedom their sexting gave her.

One stroke of my tongue across your lips and you'd go up in flames, Old Man.

Eli gulped. A real honest-to-God gulp. He was pretty close to going up in flames just at reading Beth's text.

It had been all he could do at the hospital to keep from pulling her aside and commenting on their conversation the night before. He'd thought about doing so a hundred times. He'd wanted to. He'd wanted to ask her to dinner with him, to sit and talk and get to know her. Maybe do a little shopping for tying-to-the-bed rope afterwards.

Maybe if she hadn't turned a pretty shade of pink and refused to say a full sentence to him, he would have at least issued the dinner invite. But she'd purposely avoided him. He was a hundred percent positive she'd stayed away from the nurses' station as long as she could. Was that why he barely knew her despite the fact she'd worked at the hospital for several months? He had a vague memory of her starting four or five months previously. Of seeing her in the ICU, but it hadn't really registered that he'd only seen her from a distance. Until today. Today he'd realized that it was a rare occasion that he'd directly had interaction with her regarding a patient.

His phone buzzed and he realized he hadn't yet responded to Beth's text. What would she say if he told her that her text, thoughts of her, had his entire body hard? That texting with her was the most fun, the most excitement he'd had in months? There might be something wrong with him that he hadn't been able to commit to Cassidy, but even beyond that, there had been something wrong with him that he'd fallen into a horrible life rut, forgotten how to have fun, and hadn't even realized it.

You fall asleep on me? she asked.

I wish.

Crazy, but he did wish that. Not until after he'd done a lot of other things with her but, yes, then he would like to fall asleep on Beth Taylor.

You saying I'm so boring u would doze off?

Zzzzzzzzz

I think I'm insulted.

Don't be. I'm teasing you. You know exactly what I meant when I said I wish.

What else do u wish?

That you'd pay up.

Pay up?

Don't play dumb. You know a picture is worth a thousand words.

Depends on the picture.

True, but if that picture was of you it would be worth more than all of Webster's words.

A dictionary doesn't have enough words to convince me to send a picture. Better luck next time u sext some random babe.

Eli laughed. He loved her witty comments.

I didn't text some random babe. I texted you, Beth.

I'm a babe?

Definitely. Just not random.

You intentionally texted me?

He felt a bolt of guilt. Technically, he hadn't intentionally texted her the picture. Exactly what did one say to that? He wasn't into deception, but trying to explain how he'd texted her that photo didn't even make sense to him. How could he make it make sense to someone else?

I got lucky last night.

Got lucky? Lucky would have been if I'd sent u that picture you requested.

Exactly. Quit teasing me and pay up.

But teasing u is so much fun.

He smiled and wondered if she was smiling too. He was positive that she was. He tried to picture her, lying in her bed, phone in hand, smile on her face, typing her responses to him. She wouldn't be wearing the outfit she'd described, of course, but probably some sensible pajama bottoms and top.

Somehow that thought turned him on every bit as much as the other.

If you're not going to send me a picture, the least you could do is talk dirty to me.

Okay, but just remember, you asked for it.

Even before the rapid succession of texts started arriving he guessed what she was going to do and his smile grew bigger with each message.

Mud.
Sloppy.
Grungy.
Sweaty.

Better stop, he warned. You're turning me on.

Well, don't ever say I'm not a woman who doesn't give a man what he asks for.

Remind me to be more specific next time I ask for you to give me something.

Hey, I talked dirty to u.

Maybe I should have asked you to tell me more about tying Dr. Randolph to the bed.

You did ask that. You liked that, didn't u?

I'm not the kind of guy who is into that kind of thing, normally, but you've planted a seed that keeps growing in my mind.

I think you're referring to what's growing in your pants.

There you go talking dirty again.

Just giving u more of what u want.

I want you.

You don't even know me.

True. He didn't. Yet he felt as if he did. Which had to just be lust and perhaps rebound from his break-up with Cassidy. Maybe even his mind's way of distracting him from the reality that there was something wrong with a man who couldn't love Cassidy.

I'd like to know you. Everything about you.

As he hit send, he meant every word. He did want to know everything about Beth Taylor. For a lot of different reasons. Everything about her felt fresh, new, exciting, fun.

He would know everything about her. Soon.

Beth stared at the phone and wondered at herself. Was she insane? Part of her felt insane. She was texting with someone she didn't know. Eli? Maybe. Probably.

Deep in her gut she believed it was him. Her Eli radar had started bleeping.

Yet the not knowing a hundred percent seemed to have freed her from the anxiety that overtook her when he was near. While texting she could be fun and flirty and pretend she was a sexy siren whom he should fall down and worship, rather than a woman whose ex left her self-confidence and heart in tatters.

Ask and u shall receive.

I asked for a picture.

Ask something else and perhaps u shall receive, she clarified, thinking that maybe this texting thing was just what she needed. Maybe Barry had messed with her head more than she gave him credit for. Maybe she no longer felt safe in a relationship. Maybe from the safety of texting, she could re-build her confidence in her femininity.

Favorite color?

Red. Boring question, btw.

I'm not bored. Not in the slightest. Actually, I'm so stimulated my neurons are probably in shock. I am now seeing you in a red garter and heels, btw. HOT!

You say the sweetest things.

Although she teased him, his comment flattered her. Her neurons, and a lot of other body parts, were pleased and shocked, too.

Favorite sexual position?

Yep, shocked neurons were firing away in her little brain. Fire. Fire. Fire. So how did a good girl who wanted to be bad with the right man answer that question?

Still working on figuring that one out. There's so many to choose from.

I could help you with that, you know.

There u go wanting to get lucky again.

Exactly. Okay, let's try another question. Top or Bottom?

Top. She wasn't really sure, but it was the first answer that popped into her mind so she went with it.

Leather or lace?

Depends on my mood.

Whipped cream or chocolate syrup?

Since when can a girl not have both?

Lights on or off?

On.

Because if she were ever with Eli she'd want to see him, to commit every minuscule detail about him to memory. This was a fantasy so she didn't have to acknowledge that having the lights on also meant he could see her much less than perfect body. Hadn't Barry made a point of letting her know that she was too curvy? That she wasn't tall enough, wasn't pretty enough, wasn't smart enough? Screw Barry. Ha. That's what his ex had done. In *her* bed. Ugh. She closed her eyes, took a deep breath, and filled her mind with Eli. Just Eli. The tension in her neck and shoulders eased.

Fast or slow?

Shall I repeat myself and say, Since when can a girl not have both?

Touché.

That some subtle Freudian way of you trying to tell me you want to touch me? she teased, determined to stay relaxed, to enjoy the playfulness of their texts.

Nothing subtle about me wanting to touch you. I want to touch you, Beth. All over.

She gulped.

All over?

Oh, yes. When I touch you, am I going to hear a soft satisfied sigh or a mind-blowing scream?

Either option sounded pretty darned good to her and had her skin tingling. Depends, she texted. How good are u?

Never had any complaints. Are you as turned on as I am?

How turned on are u?

Throbbingly so.

Poor baby. Need me to kiss and make u all better?

Pretty sure your mouth anywhere near me is only going to make my ache worse.

Hurt so good?

With all capital Os.

YOu bragging?

Just making a prOmise.

Of really big Orgasms?

Till yOu can't see straight.

Cause my eyes will be rOlled back?

NO, I want yOu lOOking intO my eyes when yOu Orgasm, Beth. I want tO watch yOur pleasure.

Beth's skin tingled. Her breath came fast. Her heart raced. She swallowed the lump that had formed in her throat. She was totally turned on by reading text messages. She was crazy.

That's a lot of Os. I'd like that.

Yes, yOu wOuld.

Was this Eli? Panic hit her, making her throat tighten up again. She was sexting. And wasn't even a hundred percent sure who she was sexting with. After the incident in the cafeteria and then him saying hi to her at the ICU nurses' station she believed she was texting with Eli, but what if she wasn't?

What if she was?

What about Dr. Qualls? Would they really not get back together? Could she really risk having another man walk away from her for his ex?

Sorry, but I need to go.

Tired?

Not the adjective I'd use to describe myself at the moment.

Hungry?

I'm not answering that.

It's okay, Beth. I'm hungry for you, too. Starved.

Her entire body tensed. She was hungry. Powerfully so. Needfully so. She wanted Eli, had wanted him for months.

Dream of me feeding that hunger.

I only dream of one man.

Dr. Randolph?

She didn't answer. She couldn't answer. She was so foolish. All of this was foolish. Just because she was texting in the privacy of her own home, in her darkened bedroom, with no one around to see or know, that didn't mean no one knew. Someone knew.

It's okay, Beth. I guarantee you that tonight Dr. Randolph will only dream of one woman.

She waited, somehow knowing her phone would buzz again even before she read the next message.

You.

CHAPTER FOUR

SEVENTY-TWO-YEAR-OLD Claudia Merritt watched Beth with sharp old eyes. No doubt now that the woman was conscious and feeling stronger, more able to breathe without the aid of a machine, she was tired of the ventilator tube that ran down her throat and prevented her from talking. She was vastly improved so perhaps Dr. Randolph would start weaning her off the ventilator.

Dr. Randolph. Her texter hadn't directly said that he was her fantasy man.

But he was her fantasy man.

Neither of them had specifically acknowledged his identity. Beth wasn't sure if that was a protective reflex on her part or if it was that she was afraid of asking because she was afraid of an answer either way.

How was it that this morning her patient load consisted of his respiratory patients? That had never happened before. When she'd asked her supervisor about it, Ruth had just shrugged and given a non-committal answer that had raised more questions than given answers.

Although her patient couldn't speak with the ventilator in place, Beth chatted to the woman she was checking, then recorded her stats into the computer system. She was just finishing in the room when Eli entered, looking more tempting than chocolate-dipped sin.

Just as it always did when she looked at him, her breath caught and her pulse pounded as if trying to burst free from her body.

His gaze met hers and he grinned.

Hello, heart attack. Because her heart had just stopped in her chest, leaving her feeling light-headed and giddy. Quick! Someone find that cardiologist. These days she needed him on speed dial.

She tried to respond, but was just as unable to talk as her ventilator patient. Embarrassed, hot-cheeked, and short of breath, she went to rush past him, to get out of Dodge as quickly as possible.

"Wait." He grabbed her arm, his touch gentle but causing shocks waves that must have registered around the world.

Eli was touching her! For the first time ever, his skin connected with hers. Total body meltdown.

"Stay," he said, so low she barely caught the word.

She forced her gaze upwards, stared into sparkly blue eyes that she'd swear saw into her very soul. His fingers stroked over her skin, slow, sensual, completely blocked from the eyes of their patient. Her skin goose-bumped, her core melted, her knees weakened, her brain couldn't quite comprehend that Eli was touching her.

His hot gaze searched hers and visions of their bodies doing wild and amazing things together flashed through her mind. She wanted to push him up against the wall and mash her body against his while kissing him like crazy. She wanted to rip off his clothes and kiss his throat, his chest, his flat stomach, to run her hands over all of him then hold on tight while he rocked her world.

Heat flashed in his eyes and she wondered if he could read her thoughts. If he knew how much she wanted him this very second. Every second. Always. Because she couldn't think of a time when she wouldn't want this man.

He'd texted her the night before. Had told her he'd dream of her. Hello, second heart attack!

"Don't go. I'm removing the ventilator and would like you in the room in case I need anything."

Had they been texting she'd have made some crack about knowing what he needed, but the thought only caused her face to burn all the hotter. Yowsers, the man affected her in a crazy way.

Because what she wanted him to remove was her clothes, his clothes. She wanted him to need her. To want her the way she wanted him. But whatever the heat in his eyes had been, he had gotten it under control and his attention had moved elsewhere.

Which reminded her that she needed to do the same. They were at work, the hospital, taking care of the sick, and there was a patient in the room with her. Beth so wasn't into spectator sex. Or getting fired. Focus—that's what she needed. Focus. On her patients and not on their very handsome, very sexy doctor.

He examined his patient then, while chatting to Ms. Merritt, he pulled out the ventilator tube that ran from her mouth down her throat and into her lungs. The woman's hand automatically went to her throat and she coughed.

"I put in an order for a BiPAP machine for Ms. Merritt before I came in. Will you check on the status as I do want her on BiPAP to help maintain her breathing status."

Her gaze colliding with his, she nodded. His eyes were magic, she thought. Had to be because their blue depths had her mesmerized, under his spell. They twinkled with secret messages just for her and her body zinged back its replies just as surely as if words were being exchanged. His lips curved into a smile that said he knew exactly what was happening beneath her clothes and he liked being responsible for that awareness.

"Oh, you're here." A harried-looking woman in her fifties entered the room and practically cheered when she saw Eli.

Eli and Beth didn't jump apart because they hadn't been standing that close, but the woman's interruption had the same effect as if they had. Beth could tell he wanted to say something to her, but wouldn't with others present. Just as well because she suspected her tongue had gone mute from the absolute steam of his smile.

Eli had noticed her. They'd texted the night before. He'd just touched her. Angels were playing harps somewhere off in the distance. She was sure of it.

"I was hoping to get to talk to one of Mother's doctors about her progress." Ms. Merritt's daughter's gaze went to what Eli held and she smiled. "Thank goodness that thing is out. It's really bothered her, not being able to say anything to us during the short time we get to visit with her." The woman frowned, not pausing long enough for Eli to respond and making Beth wonder if their patient would get in a word edgewise even without the ventilator tube.

"Is there anything you can do about that?" the woman continued. "The short visiting hours in ICU, that is. Thirty minutes twice a day is just not enough time with Mother when she's like this."

An older-appearing man, who was likely the woman's husband, met Beth's gaze and just gave a slight sigh as if he was used to his wife monopolizing the conversations.

When the respiratory therapist arrived to place the woman on her BiPAP machine, her daughter was still talking a mile a minute, occupying Eli's attention. Beth checked with her patient to be sure she didn't need anything then hurried from the room while Eli was trapped in the room with Claudia's talkative daughter.

If not for how her body and brain were frazzled at her encounter with Eli she could almost smile at Eli fielding the woman's rapid-fire questions, all with patience and kindness that far surpassed that of many of the doctors Beth worked with. She'd spent quite a bit of time on the phone with the woman earlier in the day, giving her an update on her mother, and knew how trying the lady could be. Eli spoke to her with respect and real concern over his patient. Beth liked that.

Okay, so she liked everything about the man. Which was the problem.

She pushed Claudia's room door closed behind her and leaned against it. Shutting her eyes, she took a deep breath. She sweated. Literally, she could feel the clamminess of her skin. What was wrong with her that just being near Eli, just having him speak to her, made her sweat?

Eli had done more than speak to her. He'd touched her.

For the first time ever his body had touched hers. Intentionally, his skin had pressed against hers. Sure, it had only been a brief touch, but her body still zinged from the flesh-to-flesh contact.

She ran her finger over the spot, took a deep

breath at the memory of his skin against hers, of his finger stroking over her. She could only imagine what her body would do if he ever really touched her, if there was lots of flesh-to-flesh contact.

Later that night Beth opened her eyes and glanced at where she'd set her cellular phone within reach of the bathtub. In hopes of a text? She'd gotten plenty enough today but none from her mystery sexter. Neither had she seen said mystery texter again after leaving Mrs. Merritt's ICU room. Because if she'd had any doubts that Eli was her mystery texter, his grin, the way he'd looked at her, touched her today had completely resolved them.

Eli had been sexting with her the past two nights. Odd really as she wouldn't have guessed him as a sexter, but, then, hadn't she been right there, sexting him back? And she'd never have thought herself capable of that either. Sexual attraction did crazy things to a person.

Would he send her hot messages again tonight?

Was it crazy that she kept checking her phone every few minutes despite the fact that she knew it hadn't made a sound? She was right here beside her phone so it wasn't as if she'd somehow missed the ding and vibration of an incoming message. But that didn't stop her from hitting the button to light the screen up just in case. No little text message icon.

Yep, she'd gone crazy.

When she'd gotten home a little while ago she'd stripped and slid into a hot, steamy, bubble-filled tub, determined to soak away the day's stresses. Still, she'd kept her phone close. Ever since her encounter with Eli she'd been on edge, wondering if she'd hear from him. Wondering if perhaps he'd track her down at the hospital and talk to her in person. Or maybe he'd text her and admit to his identity and tell her he wanted to see her in person.

But nothing. Not a single text or call. Maybe her phone wasn't working properly? Drying her pruny-from-the-water fingers with an unused washcloth, she reached for the offending silent contraption from the chair she'd pulled over near the tub so she could light up the screen yet again. Nothing. Urgh.

Maybe she should send a message to Emily just to be sure there wasn't a program malfunction. Maybe there was a cellular tower down somewhere and that's why—

Buzzzzz.

Almost dropping the vibrating phone into her bath water, Beth jerked, causing water to slosh up over her water-wrinkled skin. Her breath caught. Could it be? She hated the nervous anticipation welling within her at the possibility that the text might be from Eli. Probably just Emily or one of her own brothers, checking on her to be sure she was still alive since she hadn't talked to her siblings in several days.

Nervous, she opened the text, telling herself it wasn't him so she wouldn't be disappointed if it wasn't, yet all the while praying it was, because she would be disappointed if it wasn't.

The second her eyes lit on the number, a tightness she hadn't acknowledged eased in her chest and she let out a long, relieved sigh.

You asleep?

I can sleep when I'm old, she responded with her pruny finger.

Oh, really? Doing something fun and fabulous while awake, then?

Beth wanted to laugh. If she answered honestly she'd have to say, "Not in years." But this was some fun game she and Eli were playing and that freed her to be and do whatever she pleased. He freed some hidden-away part of her that she hadn't known existed, a part of her she had to admit she liked because he left her feeling wanted, desirable. Something that she hadn't felt since walking in on Barry with his ex.

Don't you wish you knew? she teased, moving her leg in the tub and enjoying the way the water slid over her suddenly sensitized skin. Despite the water's warm temperature, her skin prickled into goose-bumps and she wished it was his fingers gliding over her skin.

Yes, I do. Tell me, came his instant reply.

Tell u what?

What you're up to

About five foot five inches.

Smartie.

Smart women intimidate you?

Nope. I'm a guy who appreciates a smart chick.

She knew that about him. Hadn't he been dating one of the most brilliant women she knew for the majority of the time she'd known him? Didn't she expect him to eventually go back to that woman? Nope, she so wasn't going there. This was just fun between her and Eli. She wouldn't let possible future doom ruin her present.

What else do u appreciate? she asked, to take her mind off of his ex. This was fun, a fantasy. She didn't have to let reality intrude. Soon enough it would. For now, she was going to enjoy whatever this was between them because he was all she seemed able to think about. Amazingly he seemed to be thinking about her, too.

A woman who knows what she wants.

You just say that because u know YOU are what I want.

Doesn't matter how much a woman wants a man if he doesn't want her in return.

Beth stared at her phone. Just what was he saying? Doubt filled her.

Do u want me in return?

What do you think, Beth?

She sloshed her toes around in the tub, letting the lukewarm water run over her skin, but even if she dunked her head under the water, it wouldn't wash away her old hang-ups.

I think u like that I want u.

She hoped that he wasn't just using her to pass the time until he and Cassidy kissed and made up. Urgh, she was letting the future into her head again. Not good.

What's not to like about that? You're a smart, witty, beautiful, sexy woman who makes me smile.

His words echoed Emily's from the day before, making her acknowledge that she hadn't really believed her friend, hadn't really believed any of those things about herself. Not since…ugh, Barry. Perhaps there had been more truth in Emily's accusations than she had wanted to admit. She'd thought that because she wasn't pining to have the jerk back she was over him, but perhaps that didn't mean he hadn't left jagged scars in her very being. Scars she hadn't seen until Eli's texts.

Truth was, Eli made her feel sexy. Sexier than she'd ever felt. Which was crazy. How could a text conversation make her feel desirable? And smile? Because she was smiling like a grinning idiot.

Good answer, she praised his comment.

An honest answer, he replied. Are you at home?

With what I'm wearing, I'd better be at home.

Okay, you got me, came his immediate response, just as she'd anticipated. What are you wearing?

She wanted to get him.

Who says I'm wearing anything at all?

She tossed his line from the night before back out at him.

You make it HARD on a man to concentrate.

Who? Me?

Yes, you. Tell me why you're not wearing clothes. That how you do your household chores?

Beth snorted.

Right, because that's how women choose to do their housework. In the buff.

Sounds like a good idea to me. There should be a rule somewhere that says all housework should be done nude.

You're such a guy. Hate to burst your bubble, but I'm not bobbing around my house nude with a feather duster in my hands. I'm in the tub.

Would like to burst your bubbles so I could see everything in that tub with nothing to impede my view. Rub-a-dub-dub. You and me in that tub.

She glanced down at the water. When she'd first sunk into the tub, bubbles had floated on top of the water. Now she'd been in the water long enough that only a few stragglers remained. If Eli were there, would he be behind her, with her body cradled between his legs, her back resting against his chest, his arms around her while he washed her breasts with tender, loving care? Or would he be facing her? Sure, her tub wasn't that big, but this was a fantasy and in her fantasy they'd have room for all sorts of rub-a-dub-dubbing.

Be my eyes for me, Beth. Tell me what I'd see if I was there.

Beth studied her body and grimaced. Somehow she didn't think her waterlogged wrinkly skin was what he had in mind, or that an accurate description would turn him on. She wanted him turned on, as turned on as he made her.

Better yet, show me.

Shaking her head, Beth stared at the phone. She'd give him points for persistence, but no way was she shooting him a permanent image of her nudity. Not happening. If she looked like the Nordic Track girl, sure, she might consider flexing into a few sultry poses, but no fitness equipment sponsor would be knocking on her door for a photo shoot any time soon. Then an idea hit. She'd show Eli all right. She posed then snapped a photo and hit send.

Smiling in a silly way on the inside, she waited for his response, knowing she wouldn't have to wait long.

Hot! I think I just developed a foot fetish.

She laughed out loud, loving how he made her feel.

I like the glimmer of moisture on your skin, makes me want to glide my hands over you. I bet under the right circumstances you glisten all over.

Beth gulped. Okay, he'd taken her silly picture of her feet propped up on the water spout and he'd come back with something that stimulated all her senses.

Glimmer. Glide. Glisten. Ur good with G words.

Great with G words, he corrected.

Pure genius, she praised. Grand, even, she added, sending another text before he could reply.

Hey, it was my G word turn, but I always say Ladies first.

Such a Gentleman! You were too slow. Something you should know about me, I have no patience.

Gimme…

I'll slip lower in my bath and wait…impatiently.

Glimpse, he finished.
Gasp, she sent back.

Grab.

Goose-bumps.

Because her skin prickled with excitement that had nothing to do with her bubble bath.

Give.

Grinning.

Because she couldn't wipe the smile off her face. He made her feel giddy deep inside. From the inside out.

Gratification.

Generous.

Gaze.

Gymnastic, she teased, imagining her body contorted around his. Wrapping herself around him would motivate all her inner yoga moves.

Grind.

Gallant.

Groove.

Graceful.

Groan.

Glad.

The thought of him imagining them together, of him reacting, groaning from the sheer thought of it, made her glad indeed. Made her want to groan with pleasure, too.

Growing, he told her.

Gyrating.

Beth closed her eyes, moved slowly in the water, letting the water caress her skin.

Is this supposed to be turning me on? If so, good job.

How could a silly letter game set her imagination to running so wild? It was as if he was whispering each word into her ear, as if his hands stroked over her bare, wet body, as if he was there, sharing each word with her.

Grudge

Grudge? Okay, that one threw her momentarily out of her fantasy haze and she glared at her phone as if the device could explain for him.

Really? Grudge?

You never heard of a grudge…um…match? used to vent anger between a couple?

Match? Um, yeah, I know exactly what u mean and, okay, although I don't want to vent anger with u, I'll give u grudge.

She sent the text, then realized how he could read the message and went on to clarify.

Um, well u know what I mean when I say I'll give u grudge.

Although at the moment he had her so turned on she'd give him grudge any way he wanted grudge.

Golden grudge gift.

Glorious, she sent back, because he made her feel glorious, her body, her mind, her spirit.

Guided tour?

Greedy.

She doubted she'd ever feel comfortable enough to sext a photo. Not just because she didn't want a photo of herself out in cyberspace but also because to send that showed a level of trust that she wasn't sure she'd ever feel again. *Thank you, Barry, for screwing up my faith in men and myself.* But sexting with Eli was fun and sexy and appealed to her on levels she didn't even begin to understand.

Greek? Sorry I'm running out of Gs, not into Greek.

She laughed at his text.

Greek? As in it's all Greek to u? ;)

Have I ever told you that you make me smile? Or am I supposed to say "g"rin?

Good one.

He made her smile, too. So much so that her face hurt from her mouth curving so high.

Gush.

Gooey.

Globes.

Gotcha goodies.

Groan. Give greater glimpse?

"Not going to happen," she said out loud, although there wasn't anyone to hear her.

She shivered. Her bath water had gone cold some time ago. Not that she'd noticed. Her skin was on fire. Her whole body burned with desire. Their sext game had turned her on way more than she'd have dreamed possible. She'd lost her mind and was on the verge of losing her will power he had her aching so for physical release.

Stepping out of the tub, she wrapped herself in an oversized towel and stared in the mirror, wondering what Eli would see if she did snap a photo and send to him. Would he look at her hair clipped high on her head and see sexy tendrils or a tangled mess? Would he look into her desire-filled eyes and be captured by their intensity for him or would he see desperation, a woman who hadn't been able to hang onto her live-in boyfriend because she hadn't been good enough?

And her body? She wasn't some pin-up girl by any means. Just an average woman with an average body. A little too much jiggle here, not enough there. That kind of thing. Nothing horrible about her looks, but definitely nothing spectacular either. What would Eli think if she dropped her towel and sent him a photo? Not that she would, but if she did, what would his reaction be? Would he be as turned on as she was at their texting, at the photo of his abs that she'd caught herself looking at a hundred times because she couldn't bring herself to delete it, wondering if that was really him and knowing it was? Or would her phone suddenly go silent except for the chirping of lonely crickets? Would he find her "too curvy", too?

Going? Going? Gone?

Not gone. Had to get out of tub. Was turning into a prune. Drying off now.

I'm jealous of your towel. How 'bout that guided tour?

Jealous of her towel? Wow, he was good, Beth thought and dropped said towel to the floor. She stared closer at her body in the mirror. There would be no photographed guided tour. Only silly women who risked having their pictures shared with others or, worse, shared on the internet would send a "guided tour" photo. She might not be the brightest girl in the world, but she wasn't stupid.

At least, not too often.

Waiting…he sent, when she didn't immediately respond. Not wanting to turn their play into a serious talk, such as *You're going to be waiting forever, bub, if you think you're going to get a photographic tour of my body because I don't trust any man that much,* Beth sent him a teasing text instead.

What? U want more? I sent u a pic of my fabulous Passion Berry red toenails. What more could any man possibly want?

She picked the towel back up and ran the cotton material briskly over her skin, drying her moisture-slick body the best she could and trying not to think about Eli's comment about being jealous of her towel, of wondering what it would feel like if it were his hands caressing her flesh. The man sure knew exactly what to say to set her imagination afire, which wasn't helping the whole trying-to-dry-off situation.

Graffenburg? Is that a town in Germany?

Huh? Where had his question come from?

Well, is that a town or not?

I don't know. Never heard of it. Geography is not my thing.

Look it up sometime.

No time like the present. Beth pulled up the search engine on her smart phone and typed in the word. Oh, my. Oh, my, oh, my, oh, my. She should have known that one. Or maybe based on her past sexual experiences, maybe she shouldn't have. Because although she had no complaints, she couldn't honestly say Barry had ever visited that particular

German town…er…spot. Maybe he'd needed that guided tour Eli had mentioned.

Okay, so maybe I am into geography after all. You are so good for my education, Old Man.

Not that she shouldn't have known that one. She was a nurse and had studied female anatomy.

Nothing like hands-on training. You should let me show you.

Aww, are u offering to lend a helpful hand? How sweet of u.

Grateful?

I already sent you a picture of my toes.

Toes? You have toes?

She laughed at his reply, slid on an oversized Tennessee Titans T-shirt and a pair of silky panties, then crawled between her sheets.

Talented toes.

She wiggled them beneath her cotton sheets as if demonstrating.

I'll even show u my talented toes someday. Oh wait! Already did. Well, my toes, but not their talents. ;)

Lips?

Sooooo talented.

Not that she thought they were, but if her lips ever got the opportunity to touch Eli she was positive they'd take on a mind of their own and achieve things she'd never done before. The right inspiration could do that to a set of lips. She was positive.

I'm daydreaming again.

Again?

I've been daydreaming about you for the past few days. You have to know that. I want to kiss you, Beth. Touch you. To get to know you, all of you. For real. Texting isn't enough.

Beth's insides tingled, melted, grew hungry with anticipation of touching Eli's body for real. She closed her eyes and recalled how electricity had zapped her at his touch at the hospital earlier that day. She wanted that. All over.

I can't imagine kissing u. Well, I can and do, but just seems too good to be true that someday my lips will touch u.

They will. Soon.

Promise?

Oh, yeah.

Beth sighed. Once upon a time she'd never fathomed that she'd actually kiss Eli. Now? Knowing what he tasted like, what his lips felt like against hers seemed a distinct possibility and something she craved so strongly that she hated to think of the lengths she'd go to make that possibility into a reality.

You have to work tomorrow?

Not tomorrow. I finally have a day off work. Yay! J

So I won't see you tomorrow? That's not good. I will miss you.

Close your eyes and dream of me.

I can guarantee that when my eyes close, I'll be dreaming of you. For that matter, my eyes are wide open and I'm dreaming of you.

That's good.

Beth smiled. She knew exactly what he meant. She was doing exactly that, too.

Is it?

I think so. Don't u?

Yes, Beth, I think it's very good. And on that note I'm going to say goodnight, because I do have to work in just a few hours.

Beth glanced at the time on her phone. Wow. They'd texted into the wee hours.

Night… she texted back. Wondering if she should acknowledge him by using his name. For some reason she didn't want to, wanted to keep their seemingly safe little anonymous-on-his-part game going for a while longer. Silly of her, she was sure, but nothing about any of this was logical, so what did it matter, really?

Sweet dreams.

CHAPTER FIVE

"So, HE'S NOT admitted that it's him?" Emily wrinkled up her nose and not because of the smell of their favorite local coffee shop. Bennie's smelled fabulous as always with various coffee blends and pastries that would tempt an anorexic over to the other side.

As she poked the last bit of her muffin into her mouth, Beth acknowledged that she didn't require nearly that much temptation.

She'd been ecstatic when she'd called Emily and asked her to meet for a late breakfast and her friend, also off work for the day, had agreed. Sometimes a girl just needed to see her best friend first thing in the morning. Especially a morning after sexting into the wee hours with her fantasy guy.

"Not in so many words, but it is him." Mindlessly, Beth picked up her keys, toyed with them, clicked her keyless entry, and listened for the resounding beep, letting her know her car was indeed locked.

"I'm confused." Emily's perfectly drawn-on brows made a V. "Why wouldn't he just tell you it was him?"

Her horn beeped again and Beth glanced out the window at her car, not realizing she'd hit the button again. Setting her keys down on the sleek tabletop so she'd quit fiddling with them, she shrugged. "It's hard to explain, but I do understand."

It was the same reason she hadn't asked him or called him by his name.

"He told you he'd miss seeing you today?"

Smiling, Beth nodded.

"I'm still confused. If he's missing seeing you, why didn't he make plans to see you?"

Her smile faded. Yeah, while lying in her bed, thinking over their conversation, she'd wondered that too. Why hadn't he asked her to dinner or for a bed-tying session?

Then again, maybe he didn't want to rush things.

Which didn't quite fit since he'd started their relationship with a photo of his bare abs. An anonymous sext message. Although perhaps he hadn't meant it to be anonymous until she'd mentioned wanting to tie him to the bed.

"I don't know why he didn't ask to see me." Ugh.

She sounded depressed and dejected when in reality she was far from it. Emotionally, she was turning cartwheels of joy that Eli had texted her. A simple little thing really but when that text was from *the* guy, well, getting a text was huge. Enormous. Gigantic. Big times infinity.

"That's an easy fix. Ask him."

"Ask him why he didn't make plans to see me or ask him to make plans with me tonight?"

"Either. Both."

There went panic skyrocketing her blood pressure and heart rate again. Beth picked up her keys, realized what she'd done and forced herself to set them back on the table. "No, I don't think so."

Emily regarded her, no doubt taking in the heightened color in her blazing cheeks and how Beth wouldn't meet her gaze. "Why not?"

"It doesn't feel right."

"You've sexted with the man the past few nights and yet you don't feel right asking him to make plans with you?" Emily scowled and clicked her nails on the tabletop. "I don't like that."

"There's no rush. It's only been a few days."

Emily sighed. "I guess you're right, but I'm surprised at how understanding you're being about this. I'm not sure I would be. Why isn't he making a move?"

Beth was positive her friend wouldn't be patient. But every gut instinct said not to push Eli, that he would make his move when he was ready. "He's worth the wait."

"Without a doubt." Emily took a sip of her frozen mocha latte. "Do you think he'll text you tonight?"

Knowing her cheeks were flaming again, Beth gave a secretive little smile. "I know he will."

Emily's brow arched high. "My my, aren't we smug?"

Face flaming, Beth laughed. "Not smug, it's just that I know he will." She felt another vibration in her pocket and smiled. "Actually, he texted me first thing this morning."

Both of Emily's brows shot up. "Excuse me, but why are you only now telling me that? Morning texts up the game. Lots of people do and say things late at night, but a morning message, that's more serious." Her friend leaned across the table. "What did he say?"

Beth wasn't sure if she bought Emily's logic, but she'd had similar thoughts, that somehow getting texts from him in the light of day held more significance than texts sent under the cloak of night. "I am only now telling you because we were working up to that point in the conversation and I was telling you things in chronological order. We just got to this morning."

"And?"

Beth's insides practically glowed at recall of the happiness she'd experienced at reading his message. "He said, 'Good morning, Beautiful.'"

His simple text had made her feel beautiful, not too curvy at all.

"Sweet, but generic." Emily tapped her fingernail against her coffee cup. "I want more. What else did he say?"

So much for her inner glow. Emily's comment punched a hole right through Beth's giddiness. "He asked if I'd dreamed of him."

"Did you?"

From the moment she'd closed her eyes. In vivid color and detail. "What do you think?"

"That by your blush you had a very busy night. Tell me all."

Beth put her hand over her mouth to smother a nervous smile. "I'm not quite sure if I told you my dreams that you wouldn't think I was giving TMI."

Emily's eyes widened and she clapped her hands together. "And?"

"We've been texting back and forth all day. Just getting to know each other kinds of things with a lot of suggestive comments thrown in. He has amazing wit."

"Oh, this is good. Very good."

"Maybe." Beth took a sip of her frappucino, liking the sweet mocha flavor. "Like you said, he hasn't asked me out or anything. He's just texted with me in private. He may not have any plans to ever do more than that."

"I'm not sure why he hasn't asked you out yet, but it sounds as if he's going to. You need to be prepared." Emily's facial expression turned thoughtful then took on the aura of a drill sergeant. One that had Beth sitting a little straighter in her chair. "How old is the underwear you're wearing?"

"What?" Beth gawked at her friend, grateful she'd already swallowed her frappucino or else she might have spewed it all over her friend.

Emily leaned forward and stage-whispered, "Seriously, how old is the underwear you're wearing?"

Knowing that her face had to be as red as the

cherry topping on the cheesecake in the dessert display case across from their table, Beth racked her brains. "I don't know. Two years maybe."

"Well." Emily's smile was lethal. "I know how we're spending the rest of the day. We're going shopping."

Beth packed away the last of her new purchases, wondering if she was a fool to have spent so much on such tiny scraps of silk and lace. She'd always been more into practical underwear than whimsical. There hadn't been anything practical about her afternoon purchases. Ha, there hadn't been much of anything at all about her purchases period. Just expensive little triangles and strips of material.

Then again, Emily was right. If she and Eli did have a real-life encounter, did she want to be wearing old boring panties? Dream Guy Eli meet Granny Panty Beth? Not hardly.

Her phone buzzed. She grinned and forced herself to wait a full two minutes before opening the message. Couldn't have him thinking she was desperately awaiting his next text—even if she had been.

ICU wasn't the same without you there today.

Why's that?

I kept looking for you.

You knew I wasn't working today.

Didn't stop me from wanting to see you.

Emily's words played through her head. If he wanted to see her, why hadn't he made any effort to do so? Which left her stuck for a response. She had no claims on him, just as he had no claims on her. All they'd done was text with each other, fun, light, sexy texts. That might be all they ever had.

Do anything exciting today? he asked, apparently not wanting to wait on a response.

That's none of your business.

What if I want to make it my business?

Beth's breath caught. Her imagination went wild.

Do you?

His response wasn't immediate and she stared at her silent phone. Hello? Did he? Or was he just toying with her until something better came along? Or, worse, until he went back to his ex? Her heart throbbed in her throat and her pulse jittered through her body.

It's complicated, and I admittedly have some issues I have to work through, but, yes, Beth, I want you to be my business. I feel as if you already are.

She let out her pent-up breath. Complicated because of Cassidy? Issues that involved still having feelings for his ex? She wondered but didn't ask because perhaps there were some conversations that shouldn't take place via text messaging.

Are you okay with that?

His question seemed a no-brainer. On the surface. Deep beneath, where her emotions lay vulnerable, might be a different story. Could she bear being hurt again the way Barry had hurt her?

Are u okay with that? she countered.

Love your quick wit.

Just wait until u experience the rest of me. You'll be hooked.

She hoped, but was afraid to be overly optimistic outside their safe text conversation. Eli was telling her upfront that he had issues he had to work through. She'd been burned before. Barry had talked about marriage, she'd believed in him, and look where that had gotten her.

In case you haven't noticed, I already am.

Feeling as if she were freefalling emotionally, Beth shoved away her doubts. How could she not? Curling up on her sofa, she keyed in a response.

Tell me more.

You want the gory details?

She smiled.

I'm female, aren't I?

Most assuredly. Let's see. Female, that's a good place to start. Fantastically female.

Fun, she countered, because in spite of all her concerns, Eli was fun. Texting with him was fun. If she could ever get over how nervous he made her feel in real life, she bet being with him in person would be fun, too. Very fun.

Flexible?

Fortunately.

She'd always enjoyed yoga, went to Zumba several times a week, and loved sports. Working up a sweat made her feel good the way nothing else did.

Flicking?

Beth stared at the word on her screen. Flicking? As in his tongue flicking? His finger flicking? She closed her eyes, imagined his hands running over her body, his mouth kissing every nook and cranny, his tongue tracing, teasing her, flicking.

Oh, my! Her pelvic muscles squeezed at the

thought of Eli's tongue delving her most sensitive spot. She squirmed on the sofa, wanting to rock her hips to the imaginary tempo playing in her head.

Her phone buzzed in her hand, the vibration rocketing pleasure through her already sensitized body, sending a fresh wave of shivers over her.

She read his text.

Firm.

Good to know she wasn't the only one whose body was reacting to their messages. Too bad they weren't doing W because she had a few w words that aptly described her body. Wet. Wild. Willing.

Fabulous, she answered, sticking with the letter they'd been using.

Fondle.

Frequently.

Because the more he fondled her, touched her, the better. The sooner the better. She wanted him.

Flattery.

Finger.

Forceful.

Frantic.

Frenzy.

Feed.

Feel.

Full.

Feverish.

Their texts shot back and forth so fast Beth could barely keep track of who'd last texted. Her breath came just as quickly. Her heart beat just as rapidly. Her whole body tuned into her phone screen, to the words Eli sent, to the unusual foreplay setting her imagination alight.

Fiery feline

His messages made her feel that way, like a seductress, like she was beautiful and he wanted her more than anything.

Meow.

He certainly had her insides purring, wanting stroked.

That was an M. I WANT AN F.

Beth bit the inside of her lower lip, struggled with the intense need washing over her, with the reality that Eli wanted her every bit as much as she wanted him. Well, not as much, but he did want her and that was a heady sensation.

I just bet you do, she countered.

Frustrated

Yes, so was she. Horribly so. But she kept her message light, teasing.

FAKING. *grin*

Frigid?

She laughed at his fast comeback.

Fortunately not.

Flirt.

Floating.
Feet.

Fetish.

Flavor.

Flying.

Fragrant.

Fellatio. Hey, if u get to use a German town, I get to use an Italian one, she teased, amazed at herself, at their conversation, at how in sync she felt with him as they zinged messages back and forth, stimulating each other higher and higher with each F word.

Get that map, he told her.

I already Googled it. You any good at geography? Hope u didn't Flunk it, she challenged.

You'd know if I had. Fulfilled. Have I done that one yet?

No, u haven't, but I'm waiting.

She was waiting, her entire body was on edge of something big, of a huge meltdown that he had taken her to the precipice of, had her yearning for the next level that would send her into a cataclysmic pleasure overload.

See—it's contagious.

What is?

I want an F.

I think I have a bad case, she admitted, her hands running over her arms, sending tingles through her body and settling at the apex of her thighs. She repositioned herself, sliding her legs beneath her on the sofa, liking the pressure against her bottom. Is there a cure?

It's an ongoing treatment.

Frustrated—have I done that one yet?

She sent him his own words back, wanting him so much her body ached with need, so much she ached for release.

Finish, I'll help you.

Beth gulped, staring at her phone, wondering if she was reading right.

Help me?

Finger flicking fluidly.

Yes, she was reading correctly. Oh, my. Could she? No. That would be too much, would make her too vulnerable to him, would set her up for ridicule as Barry had done more than once regarding her sensuality.

Ugh on the thoughts of Barry. He was not allowed in her head. Not tonight. Not ever.

Beth? Follow my lead. Finger flicking fluidly.

Eli repeated his text.

She sucked her lower lip between her teeth. Closed her eyes, concentrated on Eli, on how he made her feel when he smiled, when he'd said her name for the first time, when he'd touched her in Mrs. Merritt's room, on how good she'd felt when he'd called her beautiful. She imagined how good she'd feel if Eli were there, complimenting her in person, touching her body with purpose. All her thoughts on Eli, she gave in to the demands of her body.

You are good at this.

Feeling fuller, firmer.

Beth gulped at the image his message put in her head, at how her body instantly responded to that image.

You have my Full attention, that's For sure. I want you.

I'm right here.

Too far away.

Breathing on your neck. Hands on your hip-bones...

I woke up this morning dreaming. You were holding my hands above my head with me stretched out beneath you. Lots of those g words were happening. Gliding. Gyrating. German towns.

Sweat dripping off my brow...

And u were kissing me. Deep, hard kisses.

Deep and hard?

DEEP and HARD.

With her last text, Beth closed her eyes and let her body burst into a prism of colors, all bright, all glorious, all Eli's doing.

Fantastic finale finding fulfillment?

No way was she going to tell him that he'd just given her the best orgasm of her life without him even being present, without him even having touched her. No way.

Only he *had* been present, encouraging her the entire way. The man got inside her head and did amazing things to her body, made her feel free, sexy.

She could only imagine what it would be like if he had really been there, had really been touching her.

Then again, maybe it was all in her head. Maybe because he was her dream guy, the guy she'd fantasized about for months, maybe that's why she'd just seen stars and had had a major body meltdown. Maybe if he'd really been there it wouldn't have been anything spectacular, because maybe she wouldn't have been able to relax, to have gotten Barry's words out of her head.

Maybe.

But as her eyelids became heavier and heavier she couldn't quite convince herself of that.

Fulfilled? he asked again.

Fatigued.

Sorry. Guess I've kept you up late again tonight and tomorrow you do have to work.

I didn't tell you that I had to work tomorrow.

I checked the schedule today. Night, Beth. Sweet dreams.

Beth was pretty sure she'd been dreaming for the past several days. Sure felt that way.

If that were the case, no one wake her up, please.

At his office, Eli flew through his morning patients with gusto.

"What's up with you this morning?" his nurse asked him. She'd been giving him an odd look all morning, but hadn't said anything while they'd been seeing patients.

"What do you mean?" Not that he didn't know. He felt more alive than he had in years. No doubt that bled through into everything he did.

"You're always pretty even keeled, but today you have an unusually good mood and can't seem to quit smiling. Plus, I heard you whistling in your office earlier. It's not as if the whole office doesn't know about you and Dr. Qualls falling out a few weeks ago. Did y'all kiss and make up?"

He had been whistling, hadn't he? Eli shook his head. "That isn't going to happen."

Eyeing him curiously, his nurse arched her brow. "Is there someone new on the scene? I can't imagine anyone more perfect than Dr. Qualls, so this new woman must really be something to have you smiling that way."

Eli fought flinching at "perfect".

"We'll leave it at life is good." That's all he was saying, because he wasn't ready to share his personal life. Not where Beth was concerned.

As crazy as it was considering he'd yet to have a single date with the woman he couldn't stop thinking about, life was good. Especially now that he was leaving the office, headed across the breezeway that connected the multi-specialty office complex to the hospital, and would soon see Beth.

Had she been as blown away as he'd been by their texting the night before? As shocked? He hardly recognized himself because he sure hadn't done anything like that before.

Not even as a silly teenaged boy had he behaved so…horny. He didn't know another word for how she made him feel. Beth did something to him. Freed his mind and burned his insides with physical need.

Crazy and not the basis for a long-term relationship, but wow on the here and now. Maybe an affair with a hot-blooded woman like Beth was just what he needed to help him figure out what it was he really wanted out of life, to help him figure out where he'd gone wrong, why he couldn't love a woman everyone told him was perfect for him. Or maybe spending time with Beth would just be fun and free him to rediscover who he was, then he could worry about his failures and his future.

He checked on all six of his current admissions, including the two assigned to Beth, but she was nowhere in sight. Had she gone back to hiding from him? Eli looked up and down the ICU hallway for the woman who had occupied his every free thought for the past few days.

There. He caught a blur of blue scrubs and brown ponytail disappearing into a patient room.

His lips curved upward at just the glimpse of her. The woman made his insides feel… He searched for the right word. Better? Lighter? Excited? Turned on?

He lingered in the hallway, passing the time by asking the charge nurse about a patient. But his brain was focused on the room where Beth was, waiting for her to come out, wondering if she'd been as affected by their sexting as he'd been.

"There's no one in that room, you know," Nurse Rogers told him, eyeing him curiously.

"Huh?" Because he'd seen Beth go in and doubted she'd slipped out without his noticing. He'd definitely have noticed.

Nurse Rogers shrugged. "Not a patient, I mean. The patient who was in the room was transferred to the regular medical floor. The tech was busy and Beth volunteered to prepare the room for another patient."

"Oh." Eli glanced toward the room, then back at the nurse. "Why are you telling me?"

"Because you're about as subtle as a ton of bricks."

He grinned at the nurse manager because he really couldn't deny the woman's assumption and she seemed to approve of his interest in Beth. To deny it would just be insulting the woman's intelligence. A ton of bricks had nothing on him.

"That smooth, eh?"

Smiling back, she nodded. "My first clue was when you asked me to assign her to your patients a couple of days ago. As many as possible. Smooth as silk."

Okay, so that hadn't been real subtle of him, but he'd wanted the opportunity to get to know Beth beyond their texting, to interact with her in person. With how she'd scurried away any time he'd been near, he hadn't been sure if she'd give him that opportunity. Fortunately, Beth's supervisor seemed to approve of his interest and hadn't been above cooperating. "A dead giveaway, eh?"

She shrugged. "About as much as when just a few days after she started working at Cravenwood she asked me to please not assign her to your patients."

Eli winced. That explained a lot and raised even more questions. Beth hadn't wanted to be assigned to his patients? "Did she give a reason?"

She shook her head. "She didn't have to."

Eli arched a brow, but rather than elaborate she just shook her head again.

"If you want details, you'll have to ask her yourself."

Right. Not that he didn't know the answer after texting with Beth. She'd felt an instant attraction to him. Lucky him. Only he'd been taken so she'd avoided him as if he'd had leprosy. How could he have been so blind?

"No time like the present," he quipped, grinning at the woman he was grateful to have on his side. "Is it okay if I occupy one of your nurses for a few minutes, Ruth?"

"I'd already told her I'd cover anything that came up on her patients while she was in the room, so no problem." She narrowed her eyes, although her smile somewhat killed the warning in her gaze. "Keep it at just a few minutes, though."

"Point taken."

Eli went to the vacated ICU room, stood in the doorway and watched Beth move efficiently about the room. Just looking at her took his breath away. How had he not noticed her in the past? She was beautiful and sexy without even trying. But way beyond the surface, she heated his blood, made him burn from the inside out, made his insides feel alive and raging with fire that needed to go up in flames with her.

When he'd touched her arm two days ago, she'd seared him to the core, turned him inside out. He wanted her more than he recalled ever wanting anyone, anything. So much so he ached with need that went far beyond satisfying a physical need.

She glanced up, acknowledged that she knew he was there but kept about her business of stripping the bed sheets.

"You don't look surprised to see me."

Without glancing toward him, she shrugged and rolled the sheets up.

"You know, this seems a little silly considering you've worked here for several months, but I'm not sure we've ever been properly introduced. I'm Dr. Eli Randolph." The man of your fantasies, he wanted to add, but she already knew that. She'd been the one to tell him, to spark his imagination, to tell him in explicit detail what she'd like to do to his body. Over and over. Sweat broke out on his brow just at the thought.

He also fought adding that she had rapidly become the woman of his fantasies. She'd brought his imagination to life, brought him to life as if he'd been walking around zombiefied.

Beth looked up again, this time a frown marring her lovely face. But she didn't speak. Not a single word and Eli fought against shuffling his feet.

"I'd like to take you out to dinner after work tonight." Or away for the first weekend they could manage to escape the hospital. Both. He wanted everything with her and the sooner the better. He'd have asked her the night before but he'd been on call and hadn't wanted to possibly have to run out on their first date.

She stopped to stare at him, but still didn't say anything. He didn't like her silence, couldn't quite understand why she didn't say anything when his insides were bursting with nervous excitement that they were so near, that her delectable body was within reach, and yet really so far away because, despite their texted touches, he had no right to touch her in person. Which irked him and made him determined to change that as quickly as possible.

"We can go anywhere you like." It had been a long time since he'd asked a woman out on a date for the first time. Years. But he didn't recall ever feeling as if he needed to convince a woman to say yes. In the past, women had always chased him.

Nothing about Beth was typical. Everything was fresh, new, and unique to her.

Still, she just stared silently at him, as if waiting for him to say some magic phrase that would trigger an affirmative from her. He'd chant "Abracadabra" or "Hocus pocus" or whatever he needed to say to get this woman under his spell. Then again, according to her texts she was already under his spell, so she should be nodding her head or leaping into his arms or something, right?

Under different circumstances, the leaping into his arms would work nicely for him. Since they were at the hospital, he'd settle for a simple "yes".

"Beth? Say something. Anything, just so long as it's not no, because I don't think I could stand it if you said no to seeing me."

"I can't." She glanced at him then rapidly looked away. "You make it difficult for me to talk."

At first he'd thought she'd meant she couldn't see him, then he'd realized she meant to talk. He heaved a sigh of relief. "Because?"

"You know."

Just like that, he did know. Actually, he felt foolish for not realizing from the moment he'd walked into the room and she'd failed to do more than acknowledge him. He grinned. She wanted him and that made her nervous, tongue-tied, shy. She really, really wanted him and it was a heady sensation to be the recipient of her desire. An honor. He really was a lucky man.

All he had to do to know that was to look into Beth's eyes, to see the emotion that shined there this very second. She wanted him to the point of flustering him and giving him thoughts of pushing her up against the hospital room wall and kissing her until neither of them could breathe, could speak, and to hell with whoever saw or gossiped.

"If it'll convince you to say yes to going to dinner with me tonight, you don't have to say a thing."

Her brows veed in pseudo confusion.

"We'll just text each other," he clarified with a waggle of his brows. "Just so long as I actually get to spend time with you, it doesn't matter. Just think, if you say yes, I could even snap my own pictures."

Her cheeks blazed red, but her eyes came alive, and she arched a brow. "From across the dinner table?"

"I'm flexible."

"I thought that was my line." She took a deep breath that sounded just shy of a gasp. Had she startled herself with her quip?

"Last night it was. I'm anxiously waiting for you to demonstrate." He grinned, liking the in-person glimpse of the fiery passion and fun that always laced her text messages. As much as how he affected her flattered him, he didn't want her so nervous she couldn't be herself. Herself was who he wanted to get to know better. Much better. "You get off work at seven?"

The beginnings of a smile on her face, she shook her head. "I'm supposed to, but it's unlikely to happen. I'm a nurse, remember?"

"I remember everything about you."

Her cheeks tinged pink again. "You don't know me. Not really."

"I'm trying to correct that, but you aren't cooperating," he pointed out, liking the low laugh that spilt from her full lips.

"I'm not a yes kind of girl."

He moved closer, so where only a few inches separated them, stared down into her beautiful face, wondering yet again how he could have seen her without really seeing her for the past few months.

Everything about her stimulated him. "That make you a no kind of girl?"

Her lips twitched. "No."

He laughed, liking the rumbling feel in his chest. He'd laughed more the past few days than he recalled laughing in years. Her silly little texts had lifted his insides. Lifted his outsides, too. "I'll be on my best behavior. I promise."

Her smile drooped slightly and she swallowed. "You know how I feel about you."

"I'd thought so, but your lack of the right enthusiastic answer is starting to make me have my doubts," he teased. He did know. He could see the excitement in her eyes, could feel the sizzling anticipation in the air between them. He could also see the fear in her eyes. Had she been hurt in the past and was afraid he was going to do the same? "I know we've texted like crazy. You make me crazy with wanting you. But tonight doesn't have to be anything more than just dinner and actually being able to see you in person rather than just in my head."

He knew she was going to go with him. He could see it on her face. He also understood her hesitancy.

"I promise I won't pressure you for anything beyond your company, Beth. Just text me your address when you clock out and I'll pick you up at your place, okay? We'll talk. Or text," he added with a grin.

Taking another deep breath, she nodded. "I'd like that."

So would he. More than he would have dreamed possible. He wanted to touch her, to pull her into his arms and hug her. She was so close. So close he could smell the soft, sweet scent of her. Not floral or overpowering, just a faint spicy sweetness. But to touch her would lead to much more because he longed to kiss her…among other things. They were at work. He didn't want to make her work life any more stressful than it had to be. He'd probably already been in the room alone with her too long.

"I'll see you tonight, Beth."

"Eli?"

He turned at the door, waited for her to say more, hoping she wasn't changing her mind.

"For the record, I can't make you the same promise as the one you just made me."

His heart thudded to a stop and restarted with a jolt. "That's okay, Beth. I'm a big boy and I'm really good under pressure."

"A girl can hope."

His gaze met hers, saw the flicker of desire burning there, and he instantly went hard. Which was a problem, considering their location. He fought crossing the room, knowing when he touched Beth he was likely to lose control completely. He wanted her so much. At the hospital wasn't the right time or place for their next touch, their first kiss.

"Text me," he said, then left while he still could.

Tonight was time enough for living out fantasies.

CHAPTER SIX

AMAZINGLY, BETH DIDN'T have to pull overtime. Had Eli somehow convinced everyone to show up for their shift and for there to be no new admissions right before shift change for once? Because clocking out at just a little past seven was a rarity and had only happened a few times since she'd started at Cravenwood.

All through shift change and giving report she'd expected something to happen to delay her leaving the hospital. Nothing had.

She exhaled a long breath and texted Eli her address and instructions to pick her up at eight. That gave her time to get home, jump in the shower, shave, moisturize and perfume herself just in case, stress over what she'd wear, then nervously wait for his arrival.

What would she wear? Would nothing at all be too obvious as to what she'd rather have than dinner? Then again, she did have all those new sexy undies Emily had convinced her to buy. Would she wear red or go with black?

Just as she got into her car, her cellular phone rang. She half expected it to be Eli, canceling. Part of her still didn't believe he could possibly feel the same about her, that none of this could be real, and that soon enough he'd reunite with Cassidy.

It was Emily.

"Need me to pinch you again?" her best friend greeted her.

At the reminder, she rubbed her upper arm, then started her car and pulled out of the hospital parking garage. "I still have the bruises from where you did earlier today."

"Well, you told me to pinch you because you had to be dreaming," Emily reminded her with a giggle, then sighed. "Oh, Beth, I'm so excited for you that he asked you out and even more so that you said yes! This is wonderful."

"It's just dinner."

Emily made a clicking sound over the phone line. "You texted the man that you wanted to tie him to your bed and lick him from head to toe. It's not just dinner."

"I never should have told you that. I didn't know

it was him when I said that, and you're making me nervous."

"No, I'm not. You were nervous before I called. You're a nervous kind of girl when it comes to that man. Since you never were in college, I blame the fiasco with Barry, but we aren't going to talk about the douche bag tonight because he is history. I called to calm you down."

"True and it's not working." She braked at a traffic light, wondering at how long the drive home seemed tonight. "Try harder."

"Beth, relax. The worst that can happen is that you realize that y'all have nothing in common, he's horrible in the sack, and you go your separate ways. You're no worse off than you were a week ago."

All true, but Beth's nerves didn't feel soothed at all.

"Actually," Emily continued, "you're better off because then you'll know rather than spend your entire life wondering if he was the one and you missed out on your chance. Plus, being with Eli will definitely put to rest any lingering thoughts of Barry. That's a big plus."

Crazy nervousness or not, her friend made way too much sense. "I guess you're right."

"Of course, I'm right."

"I don't sleep around. Ever. You know that." But she had already admitted to herself that she wanted sex with Eli. She'd admitted as much to him even. The sooner the better, so why was she whining? Nerves? Or was it just that she wanted reassurance from her best friend?

"You're not a virgin," Emily reminded her, as if she'd thought that was what Beth meant.

"This feels different." She'd been in college when she'd had sex for the first time. When she'd returned to the dorm room, Emily had taken one look at her face and known something had changed. Then there had been Barry. Barry, whom she'd lived with for several months before he'd realized he was still in love with his former girlfriend, but had forgotten to mention this until Beth had walked in on them in the apartment she and Barry had shared. After which he'd pointed out all her shortcomings and thanked her for making him realize that his ex-girlfriend really was the woman for him. Gag at the memory. Gag at the sharpness that gripped her chest.

"Randy was a decent guy you were never that crazy about but who made studying more fun,"

Emily pointed out about Beth's college boyfriend of more than a year and who had been her first lover. "Barry was an idiot who never deserved you. I never liked him. We've discussed this."

They had. At length during the conversations they'd had leading up to Emily convincing Beth to apply for a job at Cravenwood.

"But Eli is a man," Emily continued over the phone line. "A man with needs. If he wants you, count your blessings and go for it."

Go for it. It's basically what she'd already decided. To go for it. With Eli. But maybe she'd needed to hear Emily confirm what she knew because she just didn't trust her own instincts any more.

Unlike how her best friend described Beth's college flame or how she'd felt about Barry, she was crazy about Eli and had been from the first moment she'd laid eyes on him and that fabulous smile of his.

Today, he'd flashed that smile at her.

Tonight, he'd do much more than that with his mouth because one way or another she'd know what Eli's mouth felt like against hers, what he tasted of, before the morning sun rose. Deep inside she knew that to be true.

Oh, wow. Tonight she'd kiss Eli. Possibly much more than that.

How lucky could a girl get?

Then again, she'd never been that lucky.

"What if he gets back together with Dr. Qualls?" Was she whiny or what? she thought as she slowed for another traffic light. But this was her best friend so she was allowed a little whine, surely?

"Quit worrying about what might happen in the future and enjoy what is happening right now. Whether for a night or a lifetime, your fantasy guy wants you. That's pretty spectacular when you think about it."

"I can't seem to think about anything else."

"Understandable, but, Beth, you need to remember something else, too, that you seem to have forgotten over the past year."

The traffic light changed and she pressed her foot against the gas pedal, grateful she was almost home. "What's that?"

"Dr. Randolph is a very lucky guy to be your fantasy man. Never forget that or underestimate what a great woman you are. That's pretty spectacular for him too. Don't dare think otherwise."

* * *

Because she changed outfits three times, a very unspectacular-feeling Beth wasn't ready when her doorbell rang at about ten minutes till eight.

Her skirt was down about her high heels and she'd been about to kick the black stretchy material across her closet in lieu of trying on yet another that might possibly make her hips look a little less curvy and a lot more svelte. Oh, crap!

Well, that solved what she was going to wear. She yanked the stretchy material back up over her hips and smoothed out any wrinkles her indecisive garment changing had caused. Telling herself that tonight was no big deal, just a first date—with her dream man!—and that there was no reason for her to feel as if she was going to pass out, she headed toward the front of her house.

He was lucky to be her fantasy man. It was spectacular for him that she wanted him. Emily had said so. Calm. Cool. Collected. That was her. No big deal.

When she opened the door, all pretense of any of those C words vanished. Her eyes widened in surprise. Not at the gorgeous freshly showered man standing there in khakis and a blue polo that matched his eyes, she'd been expecting him and the jolt to her senses looking at him always caused, the hello, let me rip your clothes off you with my teeth, please, reaction that always hit her when she saw him. What he held in his hands was what had her jaw dropping and her yet again thinking someone should pinch her.

She rubbed her already sore arm, thinking that might do the trick but, no, he still stood in her doorway, looking like a dream come true, holding a bouquet of colorful fresh flowers.

"You look amazing," he said, his eyes raking over her body in obvious appreciation.

He made her feel amazing, as if she'd made the perfect wardrobe choice. Then again, so had he. His shirt pulled just right across his shoulders, his chest, and just beneath the material lay those fantastic abs, the image of which was permanently burned into her mind from an inches-big photo on her phone.

Her gaze went to his and she tried to hold it there because, seriously, she was in danger of ripping off his clothes, to run her fingers over those abs and memorize every ripple of flesh, to try out some of the things they'd texted, all the things they'd texted.

The man made her ache. "You didn't have to bring me flowers."

His gaze smoldering, as if he knew what she was thinking and perhaps was thinking of telling her to go right ahead, Eli grinned. "I know I didn't have to. I wanted to. You're a beautiful woman and I want to show you that I know how fortunate I am to be here with you."

There went Emily being right yet again.

Eli handed Beth the bouquet of multicolored blooms and their fingers brushed against each other. The feel of his skin against hers fried her brain and a few other choice body parts felt the sizzle. What was it about him that overloaded her senses so?

She raked her gaze away from his baby blues, over the strong, handsome planes of his face, the fullness of those masculine lips, the width of his broad shoulders, the powerful thickness of his chest tapering down to a narrow waist. There she had to stop because the flames shooting out from her cheeks just wouldn't allow any further inspection. Needless to say, just looking at him answered exactly what it was about him that overloaded her senses. Everything. Every single thing about Eli made every single cell inside her body take notice.

So that made everything she was feeling just physical, right? That was the right label for all the emotions swirling inside her? Lust. Pure and simple animalistic, instinctual lust. That's what this had been about from the moment she'd first seen him and every moment since. Lust. Yet that didn't feel accurate. Not by a long way, because surely lust alone couldn't be this overpowering?

"Thank you." She took the flowers, wondered at the moisture stinging her eyes, then turned away from him so he wouldn't see how touched she was at his gesture, how aroused she was at her visual perusal of his attributes, how confused she was by knowing deep inside that lust didn't begin to cover the emotions she felt for this wonderfully unique man. "I'll just go put them in some water."

Because she really needed to escape so she could drag in oxygen for her poor deprived brain.

Once in the kitchen, she took a deep breath, dug through her cabinets in search of a vase and finally settled for a large glass jar when she didn't find anything more appropriate. Just how long had it been since someone had given her flowers? Actu-

ally, other than dance corsages and a couple of ar-
rangements after her tonsillectomy at fifteen, she'd
never gotten flowers. Randy had been a poor college student like herself but she doubted giving
flowers had been his kind of thing anyway. Barry
had never bothered with flowers. Why should he
when he hadn't ever really loved her despite him
having told her so many times?

Telling herself not to read anything into Eli's gesture and not to do anything to his body that would
get her arrested, she arranged the flowers in the jar
and wondered at the man in her living room.

"I like your home. It suits you."

Not in her living room. In her kitchen.

She spun toward him, startled that her Eli radar
hadn't gone to bleep. Then again, her entire cir-
cuitry was pretty much shot by the fact he stood
in her house. Who would have ever dreamed Eli
would be in her house? In her kitchen? That he
would have been the first man to bring her flowers? That she'd see attraction glimmering in his
eyes? He wanted her. Whether it was just because
of their sexting or if it was something more, Eli was
attracted to her. He'd let her know in an unexpected
way, but he had let her know. Maybe she was old-

fashioned, behind the times, and sexting was just as good a way to show interest as any these modern days. Who knew?

Definitely, in Eli's case, sexting had worked. But only because she'd already been crazy about him, otherwise she'd probably have been creeped out.

She gulped and glanced away from the intensity of his eyes. She stared at his feet, liking the soft leather no doubt Italian shoes he wore with his khakis and pullover. She'd bet he looked even better without them. She closed her eyes, imagining him naked, in her kitchen. Would she have him tied to a barstool or would she be the one bound and at his gentle mercy?

Gentle. G word. All kinds of other G words popped into her head and she sank her teeth into her lower lip in frustration. Frustration. An F word. Which brought her to other F words. Which, combined with the way he was looking at her, made her knees want to buckle.

What was wrong with her? She'd had an ordinary sex life, good but nothing spectacular and definitely nothing kinky, with either of the men in her life. She'd never even thought of anything out of the ordinary until Eli. Did that mean passion hadn't ever been inspired within her?

Eli sure inspired passion. All her creative juices flowed.

Flowed. Another F word. She groaned, then grimaced.

"Beth?"

"Thank you," she rushed out, realizing she hadn't acknowledged his presence in her small but homey kitchen, hadn't acknowledged his compliment. She'd not done anything except get hung up on two letters of the alphabet. Did he feel as awkward as she did? How could she feel awkward when she'd texted with him into the wee morning hours, telling him her deepest fantasies? All of which featured him?

Or maybe because she'd shared so many of her private thoughts with him was why she felt so crazy?

"You're welcome." Those shoes and the hunky body attached moved close to her.

She looked up into blue, blue eyes. Blue. A B word. See, her brain could focus on letters besides G and F. B. Beautiful. Bold. Bite. Bite? Oh, yeah, she wanted to sink her teeth into him.

Blushing, she refocused on what he was saying. "Before we go to eat, there's something I need to do. Something I believe we both need me to do."

His fingers went into her hair, caressed her nape, giving her time to protest should she so desire, because she knew what he was about to do. Eli was going to kiss her. Her heart pounded against her ribcage, threatening to burst free. The man she had dreamed of kissing her so many times was actually going to put his mouth against hers of his own free will. Miracles happened every day.

"This." His mouth covered hers and her miracle happened.

She wasn't sure what she'd expected. Maybe it was completely normal to have fireworks explode inside you when the man of your dreams kissed you for the first time. A whole Fourth of July show was going off inside her body. One humdinger of a show. Wowzers.

His lips brushed against hers, soft, warm, and experimental, yet masterful. "You taste good."

A sound escaped her lips, but she wasn't sure if it was intelligible or not. All her brain power focused on how his mouth touched hers, on how his touch grew hungrier, more and more demanding, on how her hands had found their way into his hair. Soft. So very soft.

But not his body.

His body was rock hard.

And mashed up against hers. Hot and heavy and moving against her in ways that boiled her blood.

He felt amazing.

Better than anything she'd ever imagined and she'd imagined lots.

Her heels not giving her the steadiness she needed to keep from ending up an ooey-gooey puddle on the floor, she leaned into him, aligned her body just so against his. Her arms wrapped around him, touching, committing every sinew to memory, every ripple of his muscles, the texture of his skin, the intense heat radiating from his every pore.

She savored the feel of him, the smell, the taste, the intensity of him. This was Eli.

She was kissing Eli.

Her Eli.

She wanted him so much.

She could barely breathe, could barely hear above the pounding of her pulse, the thundering of her heart that echoed his name over and over.

"You feel good," he whispered into her neck, kissing her there, breathing in her scent and pulling her even closer. "So good I can't believe how good you feel, that I am finally kissing you."

Ha, wasn't that her line? She'd been the one waiting for months and months.

"It's only been a few days since you texted me for the first time," she pointed out between kisses, between his hands running over her body, between her hands stroking over his body.

"Seems a long time to go without touching you."

To prove his point, he tugged her shirt loose from her skirt and cupped her breast through her bra. "I don't mean to go so fast, or to put that pressure on you that I promised I wouldn't, but I need to touch you, Beth. Tell me to stop if that isn't what you want."

She knew all about that need because she felt it too. A deep need that wouldn't abate with just a few light kisses or even the passionate ones that followed. She wanted him, felt as if she'd always wanted him, that every moment of her life had been bringing her to this moment, to him.

Following his lead, her fingers found their way

beneath his polo and skimmed across his abs. He sucked in his breath, causing the muscles between her fingers to tighten. Her own muscles contracted, clenching in response to him. That photo had been him. Wow.

"This is crazy. You have me on edge," he said, sounding as if he'd been exercising intensely or was one of their pulmonary patients.

His so-real reaction to her touch empowered her, freed her nervousness to tease him much as she did when they texted, to slide her fingers beneath his waistband. "On the edge of what? Tell me, Eli. I want you to tell me. Better yet, show me."

He shivered and she marveled at how he responded to her touch, to her words. No one had ever reacted to her touch as if it were the most wondrous thing they'd ever felt. Eli did.

In the past, sex had been good. Nothing to shout out to the heavens about, but she'd enjoyed it well enough to understand what all the hoopla was about. Or so she'd thought. She hadn't understood anything, hadn't felt anything, hadn't known this intense craving, this intense pleasure.

Just touching Eli made her want to sing and shout. To Snoopydance around her apartment and squee with delight that her fingers had actually touched his beautiful belly, that she knew the pleasure of his lips against hers.

"Beth, you have me wound so tight. All I've thought about is touching you, of having you touch me. I feel like a schoolboy about to lose his mind at the slightest touch."

"Your mind?" she breathed against his throat, pressing kisses to the beat there, inhaling the musky scent of him.

"Something like that."

"The slightest touch?" Having worked his pants loose, she traced her finger over the hard ridge beneath his cotton briefs.

"Be-eth." Her name came out as two syllables. His abdomen contracted and his hands found her hips, pulled her to him and ground their bodies against each other while he kissed her mouth. Hard. Passionately. Desperately.

Really? Was this happening? her brain questioned. Was she really touching him and him acting as if she were the sex goddess she'd pretended to be during their text conversations?

Did dreams ever really come this true or had

she bumped her head and was hallucinating some fantasy world where an ordinary girl got the guy of her dreams?

CHAPTER SEVEN

ELI MUST BE dreaming. He had to be. Beth had him quivering like a schoolboy. Unbelievable. The way fire had leapt through his veins at her kiss, at her touch, was unbelievable. Never had he experienced such heat.

Never had he wanted a woman as much as he wanted this one.

She was so beautiful, so responsive to his every touch, every kiss. Her body clung to his and he couldn't get hers close enough. He wanted inside her, but his brain warned him to take it slow, that he shouldn't rush this, that he hadn't figured out his head, his future, any of those things, and that acting on pure instinct might land him in trouble. His body wanted more, faster, and was obviously in control.

He pushed her skirt up her thighs, bunching the clingy material at her waist as he lifted her onto the kitchen countertop. Not taking his eyes off the glorious vision of her high heels, gorgeous long legs, and sexy little black panties, he finished undoing his pants to where they slid to his ankles from the weight of his pockets.

"You're beautiful."

"You make me feel that way."

"You should always feel that way because you are absolutely breathtaking." His gaze locked with hers because he wanted to watch her pleasure; he pushed her panties aside and slid his fingers inside the warm, moist apex of Beth's body.

Heaven.

She clutched his shoulders and cried out his name.

The look in her eyes, the unrestrained sound of his name on her lips undid him, pushed him beyond reason, not that he hadn't been close to slipping already. Using his fingers and mouth, he brought her to climax, donned a condom, then slipped inside her.

Tight. Hot. Wet. Amazing.

He'd wanted something more, passion, to feel alive.

He'd found it and a lot more.

He'd found a woman who stimulated his brain and his body with her quick wit and her sexual appeal, a woman who freed him to do and feel more. A woman who made him smile.

He really was a lucky man.

Too bad that in all Beth's many fantasies she'd never followed through to what happened after the mind-blowing sex between Eli and her. Perhaps then she'd have some clue as to what she was supposed to say or do at this very moment.

She didn't.

Oh, she could point out that she'd sighed in pleasure and screamed in orgasmic ecstasy. Or that nothing about their coming together had been slow. They'd gone desperately fast and furious.

And lots of other F words.

Thank goodness he'd at least had enough wits about him to put on a condom. She wasn't sure she'd have had the mental capacity to remember one had he not taken care of it. She'd been that lost in emotion.

Then again, he probably had more experience with this kind of thing than she did.

Her forehead rested on his slick-with-sweat shoulder. When had they removed his shirt? Had he done so or her? She vaguely remembered clawing at the material, at wanting to sink her fingers into his shoulders, while he…

She closed her eyes and bit back a sigh.

While he'd taken her to another world.

No way had what she'd just experienced been a mere earthly experience. Oh, no. He'd sent her right into orbit and onto some other plane, some other existence, where pleasure dominated one's every sense.

But now that she'd fallen back to earth and their urgency was spent? Now that reality had set in that this was a man she worked with and she'd just had sex with him on her kitchen countertop without them even having removed their clothes other than his shirt?

They'd never even been out on a date.

She winced, mentally shaking her head at her lack of restraint. Eli's reaction to her slightest movement, to her slightest touch had given her a heady high. She had been on fire. He had been on fire. Together they'd burned her house down. Now came the ashes of their spent lust and she was mortified at how wantonly she'd behaved. She'd not even known she was capable of such complete and total release.

"Did that really just happen?" Eli's question echoed her thoughts exactly.

She nodded without lifting her head from his shoulder. She couldn't bear to look at him just in case he already felt regret. Or what if he'd found her enthusiasm a bit too much? What if he'd found her as lacking as Barry had?

As if sensing her uncertainty, he grabbed her arms and gently pushed her back, forcing her body to separate from his just far enough that he could see her face.

She wanted to close her eyes, but couldn't. The intensity in his gaze wouldn't let her.

"For the record and just so you know, you're my fantasy, Beth Taylor."

Sure she'd just dreamed everything about this evening, she blinked. "Ditto."

"What just happened…" He raked his fingers through his hair then met her eyes with his intense blue ones and grinned. "That's never happened to me, Beth. Not ever."

"Doing it on a kitchen countertop?" she asked, trying to make light of what he was saying, because she was already crazy about the man. She didn't need him giving her other ideas. She didn't need him being so wonderfully sweet in addition to being a genius on the kitchen countertop.

"That," he agreed, although the gleam in his eyes said that he could have had dozens of kitchen countertop endeavors had he so chosen. "But more than that. The having to have you."

"Oh." She wasn't sure what to say, what to admit. More than anything, she didn't want him to think she went around doing this all the time. "Me, too."

"You've never done it on a kitchen countertop before?" He grinned at her. "Must have been beginner's luck, then, because you totally owned it. You're amazing, Beth."

His praise pleased her, made her feel less self-aware of the reality of their situation and more like a heroine in a fairy-tale come true. "I just followed your lead."

"Honey, you weren't following a thing. It was all I could do to keep up with you. You set one helluva pace and refused to let me bring us down a single notch."

She had been a bit frantic with her touches, with her demands of his body. "Sorry if I was too intense. I wanted you. I feel as if we've been in foreplay for days."

"We have." Smiling, he touched her face, cupped her jaw. "Don't apologize. You were amazing. Just right. Perfect. If you couldn't tell, I wanted you too and wasn't complaining. Quite the opposite. I'm sorry if I was too rough."

With that, he leaned forward and pressed the softest of kisses to her mouth. One that was so gentle that she almost cried from the sheer tenderness.

Her gaze met his and they stared at each other in wonder.

"Do you feel that too?"

She nodded, knowing he meant the instant heat that his kiss had brought, the instant shifting of his body against hers, the instant coming alive within her body.

"Lady, if we're ever going to actually go to dinner, you'd best tell me to stop kissing you. I really didn't mean for us to do this." He grinned then shrugged. "Well, not until after we'd gone to eat, at any rate."

Food schmood. She could eat any time. Being taken to other worlds by the man of her dreams? That might be a once-in-a-lifetime moment. She wouldn't waste a single second of her time with him on mere mortal food when his body offered ambrosia.

"What if I don't want you to stop kissing me?" What if she didn't want him to ever stop kissing her? Scary thought and one that worried her because really how did one ever move on beyond one's dream guy? What if he woke up in the morning and regretted everything? What if he realized he still wanted Dr. Qualls? He'd told her it was complicated, that he had issues he had to work through. Beth fought back a burst of panic, reminded herself of Emily's words. Eli was here, with her. At this moment he wanted her, was smiling at her, was getting turned on again because of her. For now, that was enough.

"I don't want food, Eli. I want you. Over and over."

The blue of his eyes darkened and it appeared as if he was going to say one thing but then changed his mind. His gaze liquid fire, he shifted his body against hers. His amazingly aroused-again body. "Then show me the way to your bedroom so I can properly make love to you this time."

"If what we just did was improper, then forget proper and just make me scream again."

"Scream?"

"In my head I was screaming."

Leaning down and drugging her with a linger-ing kiss first, he grinned. "No worries. By the time I am through loving that delectable body of yours you're going to have lost your voice from having screamed my name in pleasure so many times. In your head or otherwise."

Hugging his waist with her thighs and digging her heels into his butt, she sighed. "Promises. Prom-ises. You're all talk and no action."

Eyes twinkling, he moved against her. "Let me remind you just how action-packed I am."

Manny Evans had worked in a factory that pro-duced glass for more than twenty years. Despite rules and regulations to prevent such things from happening, years of improper protective equipment had left his lungs a scarred mess capable of only poor oxygen exchange.

Manny had been on the lung transplant list for more than a year and if one didn't come available soon, he would slowly suffocate to death.

Due to his condition, he was a frequent flyer in the ICU. Beth had seen his name on the roster several times, had heard the other nurses talk about how much they adored him, but she had never actually been assigned to his care in the past. No doubt due to her request not to be assigned to Eli's patients.

She hadn't said a word to her nurse manager, but obviously Eli had said something because now she seemed to be making up for lost time with almost exclusively being assigned Eli's patients.

She hadn't seen him yet today, but expected him to stop by the hospital any time to round on Mr. Evans and his other seven ICU admissions. What would she say when she saw him?

Hello, Eli, thank you for the greatest sex of my life?

The truth, but not exactly appropriate conversation for work.

Not that Beth knew what was appropriate conversation for their morning after.

She and Eli had talked. A lot, actually. While lying in her bed after falling back to earth from whatever celestial place he'd lifted her to, they'd talked about all kinds of things.

Like how much he liked it when she raked her

fingernails lightly over his back, causing his flesh to goose-bump.

Like how he was a bit stunned at his short recovery time between lovemaking sessions. She'd admitted to being a bit stunned and a whole lot impressed by that ability, too. He'd attributed it to her inspiration.

Like how when he kissed her belly her nipples puckered into hard pebbles and strained toward him, wanting his attention too.

Like how much he liked how her body clung to his as they orgasmed together, which they'd done more than once despite the fact Beth had never before experienced that dual sensation.

Like a hundred other things that had seemed so important at the time but in the light of day left her wondering exactly how things stood between them. Were they a couple? Or had she just been a one-night stand?

Or a piece on the side while he waited for Cassidy to realize she'd made a mistake to let him go?

Any woman who let Eli go was making a mistake. A huge one.

Which made her wonder exactly what had happened between him and Cassidy. No one seemed to know or if they did they weren't saying. Beth wasn't asking. Other than Emily and maybe her nurse manager, no one knew something was happening between her and Eli. At least, not that she knew of. Had Eli told anyone? She didn't think so because if he had, someone would have commented, wouldn't they?

If he had, was he using her to make Cassidy jealous the way Barry had used her to make his ex jealous?

She closed her eyes and prayed not. Fate wouldn't be that cruel, would it? Eli hadn't faked wanting her, hadn't faked what they'd done, but that really was just physical.

Not that she wanted more.

Only she did want more.

Much more.

Which was a problem because who knew what Eli wanted?

"Are you new?" Manny asked in his winded way, snapping Beth back to where she was. At work. In a patient room. Checking an intravenous line. She'd been taking care of her patient totally on autopilot without the personal interaction she believed to be so important in a person's recovery and hospital experience. What was wrong with her?

Not that she didn't know. She'd been distracted from the moment she'd gotten that first text message from Eli.

"Fairly new. I've been working at Cravenwood for a few months now and have been a registered nurse for a few years." She gave him her brightest smile. "I've just never been lucky enough to be assigned to take care of you, but no worries, the other nurses warned me what a charmer you are."

They had. Manny was a favorite on the floor.

"You were lost in thought."

"Sorry." She was. She didn't like it that Eli affected her job performance. Even during the worst of times following her break-up with Barry she hadn't let her personal problems intrude during patient care, just her personal life and self-esteem. Her fascination with Eli had influenced her workplace from the moment she'd first seen him and realized he was off limits. Avoiding him had kept her sane. "You have my complete and undivided attention now."

"Manny was just teasing ya." He gave her a crooked grin. "A man?"

She winced. Was she that obvious? "What makes you think that?"

"When a woman looks that lost in thought…" he paused, took a couple of breaths "…it always involves a man." He gave her another mischievous grin. "We're a troublesome breed."

Beth gave him a small, knowing smile. "You said that. Not me."

"I call 'em as I see 'em. Men are nothing but trouble. Only thing worse than a man…" he paused again to catch his breath, waited to finish his sentence until she met his gaze "…is a woman."

Beth laughed. "You're probably right. I bet you were a ladykiller in your day."

"I'm still a ladykiller," he breathily corrected her with a twinkle in his dark eyes.

Smiling, Beth nodded her agreement. "That you are."

"Are you flirting with the nurses again, Manny?" Eli asked, coming into the ICU room and shaking his patient's hand. "I've warned you about that."

"Every chance I get, Doc." Manny held onto Eli's hand much longer than necessary and Beth noticed that Eli didn't pull away, just let the man hold on. Beth's gaze soaked up everything about Eli. The sparkle in his eyes when he glanced at her, the smile on his perfect mouth, the broadness of his shoulders, the thickness of his chest. She'd laid her head against that chest, listened to the beat of his heart while he'd dozed in her bed.

Here he was acting all normal when her insides screamed in recognition of his body, recalling the magic he wrought within her with the stroke of his fingertip. How could he just look so normal when she felt so all to pieces at his nearness?

"How 'bout you, Doc?" their patient continued. "You still chasing that purty blonde doctor or has she finally given up on outrunning ya?"

Beth's insides plummeted. She did not want to hear this conversation. Not today. Not ever.

She punched a button on Manny's IV machine that reset the flow rate, entered the data, and went to the computer to quickly document what she'd done so she could escape. She did all this without looking directly at Eli again, because if she did, no way could she hide all the emotions welling inside her body. Not the good, the bad, or the ugly green ones.

There was still that part of her reminding her that only hours before she'd had this beautiful man's undivided attention and it had been glorious. As in she'd really like to announce to the world that he was hers.

Only he wasn't.

And she couldn't. Because somehow she was involved with Eli in a relationship that no one knew about yet. Did he plan to keep their involvement a secret? If so, what did that say about her? Not that she meant anything to him. Other than a good-time distraction.

Was he just killing time with her until he went back to Cassidy, until he settled down with his ex, just as Barry had done?

"Actually, Dr. Qualls and I aren't seeing each other any more."

Beth's breath caught and she waited. Had she been wrong? Was he going to tell Manny there was a new woman in his life and it just so happened she was in the room?

Silly how much she craved Eli's acknowledgement. She didn't need validation for what they'd done the night before, yet she needed exactly that. She longed to know where his mind was, what his thoughts were about what had happened between them, what it all meant. She needed to know that all the crazy emotions running through her mind and heart this morning hadn't been ill founded.

She needed to know that she shouldn't worry about him going back to his ex-girlfriend, that he really wasn't like Barry.

"But that doesn't mean you get to start chasing her in addition to my nurses. Hands off. She's way too good for the likes of men like me and you." Eli's tone was teasing as he slid his stethoscope from around his neck, completely oblivious that he'd just poked a hole in Beth's balloon of hope.

Was that how Eli saw Cassidy? As being too good for him?

"Ha, who says she'd be running if it was Manny doing the chasing?" the old man teased, having to stop to take a breath twice in between his boast-ful words.

Eli laughed. "Lord help the female population once you get that lung transplant."

Manny gave another crooked grin. "'Cause they aren't going to be able to resist this devilishly hand-some bloke once he gets his wind back."

"Something like that," Eli agreed, shaking his head while he checked his patient. "What do you think, Beth?"

Having just logged off the computer system and preparing to make her escape so she could analyze his comment about Cassidy being too good for him and what that meant exactly, Beth refused to look at Eli but forced a smile onto her face for her patient's benefit. "I think I need to check my other patients before Manny decides to prove just how much chasing he can do now. Bye, boys."

CHAPTER EIGHT

You avoided me at the hospital.

Eli stared at his phone, waiting for a reply, not getting one, hating the sick feeling inside him that Beth wasn't answering him. He sighed.

I'm sorry if I said something wrong today.

Still no response. Obviously he'd said or done something very wrong. He'd racked his brain, playing over every nuance of the night before, of the early morning hours when he'd forced himself from her bed so they could grab a few hours' sleep before their shifts. He hadn't been smooth, that was for sure, but he'd needed her in ways he couldn't explain and sure didn't understand.

His insides had lit up when he'd entered Manny's room and seen her there. He'd wanted to take her into his arms and kiss her until she'd been as breathless as Manny.

But they hadn't really discussed how they'd handle their relationship at work and there were a lot of things they needed to talk about. Like how crazy he was about her.

While he'd been checking Manny, he'd struggled to keep his eyes off her. She was so pretty. So full of life. So exactly what he ached for this very moment.

Which had him feeling out of sorts.

And desperate. And even more confused.

Beth, talk to me.

No.

Well, at least that's something.

I don't feel like talking tonight.

Because of what happened last night?

What happened last night?

Good question and one Eli wasn't sure of the answer to. At least not the full answer. Just as he wasn't sure what had happened today. When he'd left her apartment during the early morning hours, he'd left her with a smile on her sleepy face. Then again, perhaps he'd deserved her silence for discussing Cassidy in Manny's room. As a mutual patient of his and Cassidy's, Manny knew them both and liked to tease them about each other. He'd been doing so for years. Manny had meant no harm. He himself had meant no harm. He'd simply told the man that he and Cassidy were no longer seeing each other. Was that what had upset Beth?

We made love.

He answered her question, thinking perhaps she needed reassurance. Probably only an idiot even mentioned his ex around a woman on the day after they'd had sex for the first time, but he hadn't really been the one to bring up the subject of Cassidy. And, really, he hadn't said anything out of line. At least, he didn't think so.

Had sex, she countered.

Eli took a deep breath.

If that's what you want to call it.

Is that what u want to call it?

He stared at his phone screen, ran his fingers through his hair, and sighed in frustration.

What do you want me to say, Beth?

I'm not sure.

At least she was texting with him now. It was a start. Maybe he'd been in a relationship for so long that he'd forgotten all the insecurities that came at a relationship's beginning.

You're feeling uncertain about what happened between us?

He wasn't surprised by her reply.

I guess so.

As in you regret what happened between us?

Long moments passed before his phone beeped with her answer.

Do u regret what happened between us?

Was she seriously going to answer every question he asked with a question of her own? Eli sighed again, realized that a lot of his frustrations currently came from his own insecurities, the ones that had slammed him when Beth had avoided him at the hospital, when she'd ignored his text messages. When all he'd wanted to do was take her into his arms, he hadn't liked not having any contact with her at all.

No, Beth, I don't regret our making love…

He deleted *making love* and typed *having sex*. She could call it whatever she liked. Whatever it had been wasn't like anything he'd ever experienced before.

But if you're having second thoughts about last night, maybe we shouldn't have moved so fast.

He already knew that. He'd treated her like a one-night stand. Only she wasn't. She was… He wasn't sure, just that he wanted her in his life and not just in a physical way so he shouldn't have started their relationship out that way.

I take the blame for last night, Beth. I promised you I wouldn't push you, but then I kissed you and… There's no excuse other than that I moved too fast.

I'm not sure it could be any other way between us except fast.

She had a point. He hadn't meant his kiss to send them both over the edge. But it had. From the first touch of his mouth against hers he'd been a goner, needing more than he would have imagined possible. How could he have known a kiss meant to set their nerves at ease would instead cause a nuclear reaction?

Are you saying I have no self-control?

Maybe I'm saying where u are concerned I'm the one with a lack of self-control.

For whatever it's worth, I don't regret last night, Beth. Far from it. Last night was amazing. You were amazing. We were amazing.

I agree.

Then you aren't upset with me?

Not that he didn't know she was. Hadn't she disappeared after she'd exited Manny's room? Hadn't she refused to answer any of his text messages up to just a few minutes ago?

Only with myself.

With herself? Eli didn't understand. Not her response or the way he could feel the sadness behind her words, the way he felt as if he'd move heaven and earth if it was within his power to get rid of that sadness.

I don't want you upset with you, with me, or with anyone. I want to make you smile.

You do.

You're sure?

Yes.

Can I see you tonight?

Was asking that pressing his luck? Apparently so, because she shot him down.

Not tonight.

Tomorrow night?

Ask me tomorrow.

Can I call you?

Not tonight.

What can I do?

Text me.

He sighed. He wanted to see her, to touch her, to hold her close. Obviously, she hadn't been as affected by what they'd shared. Maybe he was too tame a guy for as an exciting woman as she was. Maybe he hadn't lived up to her fantasy-guy expectations. Maybe he should have let her tie him to the bed and lick him all over. Or maybe he should have kept his hands to himself and taken her to dinner as planned.

Tell me what happened today in Manny's room.

I'd rather not.

Why?

Because there are some things I prefer not to talk about.

If we are going to have a relationship, we may have to talk about those things.

Are we going to have a relationship?

Eli swiped his fingers through his hair.

I thought we already were.

I like you, Eli. You already know that. I still can't quite get around the idea that you might like me back.

I do like you, Beth. A lot. How could you possibly think otherwise?

Curled beneath a blanket on her sofa, Beth stared at her phone. What was she doing? Eli must think her an emotional mess. She *was* an emotional mess. An emotional mess that needed him.

How could she explain how he made her feel? How Barry had destroyed her self-image? How she was terrified of getting hurt?

She wished she could make her insecurities disappear completely. Then again, she was only human. Female human. He'd been discussing his ex-girlfriend being off limits with another man. Surely that allowed her a little green-eyed leeway?

How could she not be a little green-eyed when Eli hadn't volunteered to tell Manny that, no, he wasn't chasing the beautiful blonde doctor because he was busy chasing short dumpy Beth? When, as far as she knew, he hadn't told anyone? Okay, so apparently he had talked to her nurse manager to have her patient load shifted to include his patients but, really, what was that in the grand scheme of things?

Despite whatever jealousy and uncertainty she'd felt, his persistence in texting her since the incident soothed something within her. So why hadn't she let him come over? Because she was afraid he'd leave her for Cassidy, the way Barry had left her for his ex? Because hearing Eli discuss Cassidy had brought home her biggest fear and she'd gone into defensive mode?

Beth, talk to me.

He probably thought she'd gone back into silent mode.

I'm sorry, Eli. This is difficult for me.

Talking to me?

You already know that my vocal cords refuse to co-operate when I'm near you, but that's not what I meant.

You didn't have trouble talking to me last night.

No, she hadn't. She'd amazed herself at how vocal she'd been with him, telling him what she wanted, what she liked, how her body felt when he touched her. Never had she felt so free, so completely in sync with someone. So why couldn't she just tell him her fears?

That was different. That was physical. Sharing my emotions is harder.

She realized that sounded as if she devalued what had happened between them and she quickly clarified.

I've only been with two men, Eli. My first was a boyfriend in college. The second was a man I'd planned to marry.

Tell me about him.

Barry?

She so didn't want to tell Eli about Barry. What good could come from telling your fantasy guy that a man who wasn't worthy of shining his shoes had found you lacking?

He's the man you planned to marry?

Yes. I'm not sure what you want me to tell you.

Whatever you want to tell me about him. Tell me why he's no longer in your life so I can be sure not to make the same mistakes he made.

She took a deep breath and went with the bare facts. Literally.

He had sex with his ex-girlfriend in my bed.

Eli stared at his phone. Hell. No wonder Beth had clammed up when he'd talked about Cassidy.

I'd never do that to you, Beth.

I'd never give you the chance to.

Eli frowned, trying to decipher what she meant. That she'd never let a man get that close to her again? That she was some crazy stalker chick who would go psycho on him if he tried to get back with Cassidy? Instinctively, he knew Beth would never hurt anyone, regardless of how that person might have hurt her. Which meant that she'd erected walls to protect her heart.

I can't believe I just told you that.

I'm glad you did.

Why?

It helps me to understand you better.

I'm not sure that's a good thing. I'm a mess.

Just because you had your heart trampled on doesn't make you a mess, Beth. It just means you cared and your Barry was an idiot.

Just thinking about the man, about him having hurt Beth, made Eli want to track the guy down and return the favor but in a more physically painful kind of way.

That's what Emily says, but that I believed in him, that I let him hurt me, makes me feel like I was the idiot.

I'm sorry you hurt, Beth, but I'm not sorry that he's not in your life any more. Actually, I'm grateful for what he did because his mistakes brought you to me, didn't they?

Her moving to Cravenwood had been the direct result of her ex's treachery. Her being single, available to be a part of his life, was a direct result of that treachery. He'd never choose for Beth to hurt, but he could only be grateful that the idiot she'd lived with hadn't been man enough to hold onto her.

Yes. It all happened about a year ago. When Barry got engaged around six months ago, I let Emily convince me to move here. I just needed to get away and start over somewhere I didn't have to constantly see him.

Because she couldn't bear to see the man she loved with someone else? The thought of her car-ing for another man, anyone other than him, didn't sit well.

Are you still in love with him? Eli asked, not sure if he wanted to know the answer, wondering why the muscles around his ribcage contracted to the point he could barely breathe.

No. I'd never have had sex with you if I was in love with another man. That isn't who I am.

Great answer.

He pulled in a deep breath, slowly blew it out, wondered what was happening to him that he was so caught up in a woman he'd known for such a short time.

The truth. How is it this started about your ex and ended up being about my ex?

I suspect it's because your ex influences how you view my ex.

Probably.

Cassidy is no threat to you.

She's smart, beautiful—perfect, really.

Perfect. He closed his eyes.

I thought so once upon a time.

You said she was too good for you today.

Had that been what had upset Beth?

She is.

Not through my eyes.

Thanks, but she really is a much better person than me all the way around.

Did you end things or did she?

I did.

Why?

How did he explain what he didn't fully understand himself? That although, yes, Cassidy was perfect, she wasn't perfect for him.

I wanted my relationship to work with Cassidy. She's a wonderful woman. My parents adore her, but ultimately I just didn't want the same things she wanted.

Which were?

Marriage. Kids.

You don't want marriage or kids?

Suddenly he couldn't breathe again.

I do want those things, but no matter how much I tried to see myself growing old with Cassidy, I couldn't envision it.

If someone as amazing as Dr. Qualls couldn't inspire you to envision marriage and kids, perhaps you really aren't looking to settle down yet.

Perhaps not.

He admitted that, although he knew that had Cassidy been the right woman he wouldn't have hesitated to propose.

At least, he didn't think so. Wasn't that what he'd been struggling with on the night he'd first texted Beth? That he couldn't be content with a perfect woman and that there must be something wrong with him? That Cassidy was the best woman he'd ever known and yet she hadn't been enough. What did that say about him?

What are we, Eli?

I'm not sure.

I can't sleep with you if you're going to be seeing other women.

I'm not seeing other women and have no plans to.

Plans change.

If my plans change, I'll tell you.

I'd want you to.

Beth, I won't sleep with another woman while you and I are seeing each other.

He couldn't even fathom wanting another woman. Couldn't fathom not having Beth in his life. Crazy since Cassidy had been in his life years and yet he knew he'd miss Beth in ways he didn't miss Cassidy.

All I can think about is you.

I know the feeling. I wake up thinking about you and go to sleep thinking about you.

And in between?

I'm thinking about you.

I like that.

It scares me.

Scared him, too, because he didn't understand it. Was he going through some kind of mid-life crisis? Some kind of rebound to his break-up with Cassidy?

Don't be afraid of me, Beth.

Don't hurt me.

I'll do my best not to.

He would. Crazy, but he felt protective of Beth, as if he wanted to fight her dragons and be the hero who saved her time and again.

Don't hurt me either.

He wasn't sure where the plea had come from, but it was a plea, a heartfelt one, which made him wonder why he felt so vulnerable to Beth.

Ha. As if I could.

You might.

How insane he'd felt when she'd shut him out this afternoon gave testimony to the power she already held over him.

I won't. It'll be you who ends our relationship.

You can't know that.

Sure I do. You ended your relationship with Dr. Qualls. I don't fool myself that u won't do the same with me.

You aren't Cassidy.

Exactly. I'm not perfect.

Beth, from my perspective, that's a good thing.

I can't see how.

Because you aren't looking through my eyes.

Then you must be blind.

He smiled.

There goes that sharp wit I adore.

So u say.

Can I see you tomorrow, Beth?

Depends. You working?

I am.

Then you'll no doubt see me.

No doubt I will. Night, Beth. Think about me.

No doubt I will. Night, Eli.

CHAPTER NINE

BETH ASSISTED THE respiratory therapist to fasten a pulmonary vest onto her chronic obstructive pulmonary disease patient who'd been admitted the day before with pneumonia. She adjusted the settings to provide a gentle but effective pounding against the patient's back to break up mucus in his diseased lungs.

No doubt Mr. Gunn would be transferred to the medical floor later that day if his vitals continued to improve as they'd done throughout the night.

No wonder, with Eli as his doctor.

Nope, she so wasn't going to let her mind go to Eli while she was at work. Still, her face flamed as her mind went exactly to Eli. To their texting the night before. She couldn't believe she'd opened up to him, told him about Barry, that she'd essentially admitted to him that she knew he'd eventually hurt her. He'd texted all the right things back, of course. Then again, Barry had always said the right things to her. He'd claimed to love her right up until she'd walked in on him with his ex.

Eli didn't claim love. Surprisingly, their messages hadn't gone physical the night before. She'd expected them, to, really, because wasn't that what their relationship was based on? Sex?

Perhaps, but perhaps there was more. Then again, Dr. Qualls hadn't inspired him to want more, so why did she think she had a chance of him wanting more with her?

But rather than worry about that, she'd take one day at a time, enjoy that for now Eli wanted her and, regardless, tomorrow would take care of itself. Living one day at a time was all one could really do anyway. One could make all the plans in the world but could only carry out those plans in the actual moment.

"This thing is a torture device, you know?" her patient commented, causing Beth's gaze to lift to his as she adjusted the vest's strap.

"I know," she agreed.

"Figure it's me who should look like I was taking a beating, not you," her breathy patient mused, eyeing her curiously. "But I'd bet money you had a more tortured look on your face than was on mine."

"Probably so. Maybe we don't have your settings high enough," she teased, giving the older man a pointed look then glancing toward the therapist. "What do you think? Should we crank him up a few levels?"

The therapist laughed and nodded her agreement.

With a grin on his wrinkled face their patient nodded his understanding. "I see how it is. You two pretty ladies ganging up on a poor, defense-less man while he's down on his luck."

"I'm sure you do see exactly how it is," Beth agreed, patting his hand in feigned commisera-tion. "Now, you settle down and do your therapy."

"I'll see you a little later, Mr. Gunn," the thera-pist promised, waving goodbye to them both and then leaving the room.

After a few minutes during which Beth was on the computer, logging in his vitals and her nurse's note, he sighed. "Not much therapy when I just have to sit here, letting this contraption beat the crap out of me."

"Mucus," she corrected, giving him a teasing wink and signing off the electronic chart. "Mucus is what it's supposed to beat out of you. Not the other."

"I'll keep that in mind," he said, his laughter leading to a coughing spell. When he had difficulty clearing his airways and his oxygen saturation dropped to the low eighties, Beth grabbed a suction kit and aided him with the removal of the mucus, thinking that if his numbers didn't rise significantly, she'd be calling the respiratory therapist back into the room.

She glanced at his oximetry readings and was glad to see his oxygen level had risen to eighty-nine percent. Not great and not where she wanted his numbers to be running, but, unfortunately, not far from his baseline either.

"Hey, Mr. Gunn, Beth," Eli greeted him on entering the room, hoping the pounding of the man's pulmonary vest drowned out the thudding of his heart at seeing Beth.

When her gaze met his and she smiled, full-blown smiled with it reaching her blue-green eyes, everything in him came to a screeching halt, including the thud of his heartbeat.

"Am I glad to see you," she greeted him, and all her body language screamed it was true. "Mr. Gunn here decided to cough up a lung just a bit ago."

Hmm, was her joy at seeing him just professional? No. Her gaze searched his, spoke volumes, told him she really was glad to see him, that perhaps she'd missed him as much the night before as he'd missed her.

"Ain't my fault if this contraption done pulverized my insides." Mr. Gunn went into a coughing spell to emphasize his point.

Eli shot a quick wink at Beth as he moved to Mr. Gunn's side. "I came in here to listen to your lungs, but I can hear the junk still in there and I'm not going to remove the vest since you've just started the treatment. I'll come back by when you've finished and have a listen then." He turned to Beth, who hadn't left Mr. Gunn's side. "Go ahead and give him another round of Solu-Medrol via IV and have the therapist give another nebulizer treatment."

Beth verified the steroid dosage for the intravenous infusion and which inhaled medication Eli wanted given in the nebulizer. He nodded then turned back to his patient while Beth put his orders into the man's electronic medical record.

"We'll have you breathing easier soon," Eli assured his patient.

"I hope so, Doc."

He moved so he could see the computer screen where Beth entered the medication request to be sent to the pharmacy. He was so close he could practically feel her body heat. Whether it was his imagination or reality, her light fresh fragrance filled his nostrils, making him want to inhale deeply, making him want to close his eyes and just remember.

She turned, coming within inches of his body, and glanced up at him. "Excuse me, Dr. Randolph."

Her lips twitched and his entire body throbbed to feel that flutter against his mouth. He wanted her. Pure and simple, he wanted Beth.

His mind filled with the night he'd spent in her arms. In her kitchen. In her bed. It wasn't enough. Not nearly enough. He wanted more.

"Go out with me tonight."

"Dr. Randolph?" Her eyes widened, obviously shocked that he'd asked her in their patient's room.

Yesterday she'd gotten upset that he hadn't acknowledged her role in his life. That wouldn't be the case today.

"You heard me."

She glanced behind him at their patient, who was eyeing them curiously and making no pretense otherwise. "I'm not sure this is an appropriate time for you to be asking me that."

"Sure it is. There's no time like the present, right, Mr. Gunn?"

"Right." The man cackled, obviously enjoying being privy to their conversation. "Would be mighty embarrassing for the doc for you to shoot him down in front of one of his patients."

Eli nodded in commiseration with the man's observation. "Mighty embarrassing. Might be impossible to recover."

Beth rolled her eyes and shook her finger playfully at Mr. Gunn. "You're supposed to be on my side."

"Nah," the man disagreed. "We men have to stick together."

Beth laughed. "I should have known."

"Is that a yes?"

Meeting his gaze, her lips curved upwards and he knew that, despite her scolding, he'd done the right thing. "What do you think?"

"That you are going to text me when you get off work?"

Her smile widened and she nodded.

He watched her leave the room, liking the slight

sway of her curvy hips, liking the warmth emanating through him at her smile, at the knowledge that tonight he wouldn't have to text her from his lonely bedroom. Tonight he'd be with Beth and even if all he did was hold her hand, just being with her would be enough. If more than that happened, well, okay, he'd be honest, if they were alone together, more than that would likely happen. His body went a little crazy around Beth.

But it was a good crazy.

"What a woman," he told the older man lying in the hospital bed.

"I thought you were dating some fancy doctor."

"I used to."

"Not any more?"

"Obviously not."

"That one there reminds me of my Lucy. A real firecracker. Not that she knows it. But some lucky man is going to light her fuse and get to see one heck of a show."

"Sounds scary."

The older man gave a so-what look. "Relationships aren't for the faint of heart."

Eli laughed and patted the man's vest-covered shoulder. "Isn't that the truth?"

* * *

"I'm sorry we couldn't leave earlier," Beth apologized two weeks later for what had to be the twentieth time since they'd climbed into Eli's car. Despite having worked all day, excitement flowed through her veins at their plans.

Eli glanced toward her, the glow of the luxury car's instrument panel lighting up his handsome face. "Not a problem. I knew we'd have to wait to leave until you got off your shift."

"I seriously wouldn't have minded if you'd just picked me up from the hospital so we could have left directly from there." She'd wondered why he hadn't since it would have saved them about thirty minutes.

"Your car would have sat at the hospital all weekend if I had. We're not in that much of a rush."

Had he worried about people gossiping? Or was it more about Cassidy possibly hearing that he'd gone out of town with her?

Since she'd opened up to Eli about Barry, Beth had forced thoughts of the doctor from her mind, had carried on at the hospital as if nothing was different when she worked next to the woman, had pretended that she wasn't worried that dating her wasn't going to make Eli realize that he'd had the perfect woman for him already. She'd mostly succeeded. She wouldn't start failing now. Not at the beginning of their weekend away together.

A weekend away with Eli. Wasn't that what she'd sort of requested on the first night they'd texted? Wow, but that seemed so long ago. Trying to recall a time when her world hadn't revolved around Eli seemed impossible.

"Speak for yourself," she replied to his comment about them not being in a rush.

He glanced her way again and laughed. "I hope you're not disappointed. It's just a small cabin in Gatlinburg."

Didn't he realize a weekend away with him was a fantasy come true? That he was what she was excited most about? But she was excited about their trip, too.

"I've not been to Gatlinburg since I was a small girl and my family went there. It was one of the few vacations we went on." It was a good three hours away from home, but he'd asked her to go away with him for the weekend and she sure wasn't going to say no.

"Tell me about your family," he encouraged,

pulling onto I-40 to head east toward the Smoky Mountains.

Beth did. She told him about her brothers, her parents, about family get-togethers, and the pranks they pulled on each other. She told him about different childhood memories, high-school memories, about meeting Emily in her freshman year of college and how they'd become fast friends. She even told him a little more about her relationship with Barry. The abbreviated version, of course, but she told him. Amazing what one could reveal during a three-hour-plus car drive.

"So this guy you lived with, the one who cheated on you, he's engaged to be married now?"

Beth nodded then realized his eyes were on the road as they zoomed through the late-night Knoxville traffic, which consisted mostly of eighteen-wheeler trucks, and then said, "For all I know, they're already married. I haven't kept up with him since I moved to Cravenwood. What about you? Any serious relationships prior to Dr. Qualls?"

"A few that stand out from high school and undergraduate, but none that lasted more than a year until Cassidy."

Cassidy. Beth's insides pinched involuntarily.

They hadn't discussed his ex nearly as much as they had hers. She didn't want to talk about Cassidy, yet she did. Part of her needed to know how he felt about the beautiful doctor, what about her had made him believe they didn't have a future together? She sucked in a deep breath and went for it. "How did you meet her?"

"Mutual friends during medical school," he answered, sounding casual, as if her question, his answer were no big deal. "We kept being at the same social functions, the same study groups, and frequently we'd be the odd man and woman out. I suppose it's natural that we migrated toward each other."

She digested that. "So it wasn't love at first sight?"

He laughed. "Not by any stretch of the imagination. More mutual admiration and respect for each other. Everyone kept telling us we were perfect for each other and meant to be together and then we just were."

"She's very beautiful." Why she pushed she wasn't sure, maybe just to see his reaction to talking about Cassidy. Regardless, she didn't want to fight with him, not on their weekend away together, so if he didn't respond, she'd just let the topic go.

"Yes, she is a beautiful woman, and so are you. I'm a lucky man."

"Thank you," Beth told him, staring out the front windshield with her hands in her lap. She wasn't quite sure what to say beyond that. She didn't want to be jealous, didn't want to think about his ex-girl-friend, yet the woman popped into her mind way too often. As a defense mechanism or because of some real sense of impending doom?

"She and I aren't going to get back together, Beth."

Had he read her mind?

"After you telling me about your ex, I understand why you would be cautious, but you have nothing to worry about on that score. Cassidy is my friend now. Nothing more."

"Okay," she answered, because, really, what else could she say? She hoped he was right. "I'm sorry. I really don't have a right to ask you about her."

He glanced toward her, frowned. "Surely you don't believe that?"

She bit her lower lip.

"Beth, we've been having sex for the past two weeks. We're going away for the weekend. You have a right to ask me about things that concern you. I expect you to. I want you to."

She reached across the car console and touched his thigh. Not a sexual touch, just one of comfort and care, although that tingle of awareness was always there. "Thank you."

"For?"

"Being in my life."

He placed his hand over hers, gave her a reassuring squeeze, then lifted her hand to his lips, and kissed her fingers. "No, Beth, thank you for being in mine. Like I said, I'm a lucky guy."

The cabin turned out to be even better than it had looked online when Eli had reserved it. He'd paid more since it had been a last-minute reservation and they were in the middle of fall leaf season, but the look on Beth's face had been well worth the expense.

A weekend alone with Beth when he could fall asleep next to her, wake up next to her, and spend two whole days with her without worrying about anything beyond the two of them. He couldn't think of anywhere else in the world he'd rather be.

"Eli, this is marvelous!" She spun around in the

rustic living room that was open to the kitchen and dining area. Bear carvings and photos were scattered around the room and there was even a fake bearskin rug on the floor.

Visions of Beth, naked and arching into his touch while laid out on that rug, filled his mind. Instantly, his pants tightened.

He wanted her. He always wanted her. Couldn't look at her without getting turned on. He at least needed to unpack the groceries they'd stopped and bought in Sevierville prior to stripping Beth naked. Maybe, just maybe, he could hold out that long. Maybe.

When he didn't respond to her comment, her gaze followed his and she grinned. "I know what you're thinking, Eli Randolph."

"And I should be ashamed of my dirty thoughts?" he asked, moving to her and taking her in his arms, looking down into her smiling face and thinking he really was the luckiest guy in the world.

Especially when she shook her head.

"Nope." Her smile served as a flame, lighting fires all along his nerve endings. "I like what you're thinking. It's what I'm thinking too."

"You are?" He swallowed the lump forming in

his throat and decided the groceries could wait. The night air was just brisk enough they wouldn't quickly ruin.

Beth nodded, rubbing her body against his, hardening him to epic proportions. "I can't wait to see the bedroom. You think there's a fireplace in there, too?"

"Let's go find out." With that he scooped her into his arms and carried her through the small cabin toward what he hoped was the bedroom, because either way it was the room where he was going to strip off Beth's clothes and kiss her all over.

Waking in Eli's arms was a new experience for Beth. Sure, he spent most every night in her bed for the past two weeks, but he'd always left before dawn. Today they had nowhere they had to be other than with each other. It was a marvelous sensation to wake up, realize he was next to her, his arm draped over her body possessively. She liked it.

So much so she hated to let on that she was awake because it would mean leaving the warm comfort of their bed. Slowly, she lifted her eyelids to welcome the day and soak in the vision of Eli next to her.

"Good morning, beautiful."

Beautiful wasn't the right adjective to describe her first thing in the morning, but Eli looked at her as if she really was beautiful so she didn't argue. Instead, she glowed on the inside over his words, the same words he'd texted her every morning the past two weeks. He might not have been there when she had woken up, but he had texting her first thing down to an exact science.

Apparently, he'd been awake for some time and had been watching her sleep. Great. She hoped she hadn't snored, snorted, or made some other more embarrassing body noise.

"You should have woken me."

He shook his head. "No way. I've been enjoying the view."

She rolled her eyes. "If you had woken me we could have been outside, enjoying the view for real."

"The view will still be there when we do finally make it outdoors and nothing out there could ever compete with you."

Warmth spread through Beth. "You sound like it might be a while before we make it outdoors."

He reached out, touched her face, stroking his fingers over her cheeks and starting fires all through her body at his gentle touch. "Just a guess."

She turned to where her lips brushed his fingertips and she kissed them. "I'd say more of an educated assumption."

"I try not to make assumptions where beautiful women in my bed are concerned."

"Have that problem often?"

He shook his head. "Not as often as you might think."

"I'm glad. I want to be the only woman in your bed."

"You are the only woman in my bed."

She didn't clarify that she meant forever. To do that would mean actually acknowledging that fact herself and she wasn't ready to do that. Besides, he probably already knew. After all, he was her fantasy guy.

Much later, they cooked breakfast together, laughing, talking, playing, and touching frequently while they moved about the kitchen.

When they'd eaten the scrumptious omelets, Eli helped clear their dishes, a bit amazed at how in sync they were, at how efficiently they worked together. Then again, he should have known. Weren't their bodies amazing together? Why should he have expected this to be any different?

"What would you like to do today?"

"Just so long as I'm with you, I'm good." The smile on her face said it was true. Just being with him made her happy. Which made him happy. Because just being with her made him happy, too.

He didn't feel the need to entertain her, to make sure she wasn't bored. Just being together was enough. He liked that a lot.

Her smile was contagious and spread to his face.

"That's way too easy," he mused.

She wrapped her arms around his neck and smiled up at him. "That doesn't make it any less true."

He agreed. Lots of things felt easy with Beth. Being himself, not feeling any pressure to be more than who he was, just going with the moment and feeling. He wrapped his arms around her waist, smiled down into her lovely face, thinking he'd have to make it a priority to kiss each and every one of the light freckles that dotted her nose. Never had he felt so giddy on the inside. Or so absolutely turned on by a woman.

"I'm crazy about you, Beth. I hope you know that."

He wouldn't have thought it possible, but her smile broadened. "Thank you, Eli. I hope you know that I'm crazy about you, too."

"Uh-oh."

"What?" she asked, her eyes filling with feigned concern because she could obviously feel exactly what his problem was.

"I just realized something."

"What?" She moved against him, her body brushing against what he'd realized.

"I no longer want to go anywhere except back to bed."

Her lips twitched. "That's odd. That's exactly where I was hoping to go first." She stood on tiptoe and pressed a light kiss to his lips. "And second." Another kiss. "And third…"

Eventually they left the cabin. Eli drove them out of their mountain alcove to downtown Gatlinburg. They parked the car in a paid parking lot so they could walk along the quaint shops. They went through several gift shops.

"Have you been in the aquarium?" he asked when

they stood outside the large building, trying to decide what to do next.

"No, we never made it here when I came with my family." She gave him a puppy dog eye look. "I always wanted to go."

"Come on." He tugged on her hand and, laughing, they headed up the winding deckway to the entrance, where he bought tickets.

They went through the aquarium, marveled over the shark tank they traveled under on a conveyor belt, and then petted sting rays.

When they finished, hand in hand they resumed their walk along the strip, stopping to peer in one shop or another and occasionally going inside. Currently, they stood inside a candy shop, watching taffy be made.

"I remember watching this when I came here with my family," Beth mused, her eyes glued in fascination at the machine pulling the taffy. "My parents bought us a box and my brothers ate almost all of it before we'd even made it back to the car. They'd make silly faces with the taffy stuck to their teeth."

Unwrapping a sample piece of taffy, Eli's eyes were glued on her, in just as much fascination, he was sure. Her eyes were joy lit and her smile was genuine.

So was his. He couldn't recall feeling as at peace as he did when he was with Beth. Which was crazy because he was also in a constant state of need when he was around her, which wasn't peaceful in the slightest.

"What?" she asked, catching him staring.

"Nothing," he told her, leaning forward and kissing the tip of her nose. "Just you."

"What about me?"

"Everything, Beth. Everything about you." He popped the candy into his mouth.

"Is that a good thing?"

Taffy stuck between and on his teeth, he grinned. "Oh, yeah."

Laughing out loud, she smiled back at him. Pink taffy clung to her teeth. Her eyes twinkled. "O?"

"Woman, you are insatiable," he accused, linking his hand with hers and attempting to clean the candy from his teeth with his tongue.

"Only where you're concerned," she admitted.

"Good answer."

"Honest answer," she said, squeezing his hand. "I've never felt the way you make me feel, Eli."

His heart swelled. "I know just what you mean. I feel the same." He lifted her hand to his mouth, kissed her then tugged her toward him. "Come on. Let's go find something to eat then we'll go back to the cabin."

"And you accuse me of being insatiable."

Beth stared at herself in the bathroom mirror. She wasn't sure the red lace outfit she wore exactly fitted with the rustic décor of the cabin, but it's what she'd packed. She and Emily had gone for another shopping trip this week after Eli had asked her to go away for the weekend and Beth had had one specific goal in mind. To find the red outfit and heels she'd described to Eli during one of their first texting sessions. She'd known immediately when she'd seen the lacy get-up that she'd be buying it.

So why was she standing in front of the mirror, freshly showered, shaved, moisturized and ready to go find her man, yet procrastinating?

Last night, this morning, all day had been wonderful. No doubt tonight would be wonderful, too. Tomorrow they'd wake up together, cook breakfast together again, pack up their belongings, do the touristy thing—he'd promised to take her to one of the photo booths and take a cowboy/saloon-girl shot with her—then drive home. Then what?

Then what did she want to be then what? She didn't even know.

She shouldn't feel as if her very being was tied up in Eli.

Yet she did.

She wouldn't think about what that meant, wouldn't label the emotions she felt for him. Instead, she'd go into the other room and surprise him with her outfit. Then she'd show him everything in her heart, even if she wasn't ready to say the words out loud.

Eli aimed the remote control at the flat screen and flipped through the channels until he found a recap of the day's football games. He enjoyed sports, but couldn't focus on the numbers and plays flashing across the screen.

All he could think about was the woman in the cabin with him. They'd had a great day. A wonderful day that would always stand out as special in his mind.

Everything about her felt right. Her smile, the way she looked at him, the way she kissed him, the way her hand fitted so perfectly with his, the way she made him laugh.

He wanted this when they got back to Cravenwood.

Although he certainly hadn't been trying to keep his developing relationship with Beth a secret, he hadn't advertised it either, and he knew why.

He didn't want Cassidy hurt that he'd so quickly moved into another relationship. He hadn't intended to find someone else so quickly, hadn't even been looking when he'd accidentally texted Beth, but now that he'd found her, he wasn't going to let go. He wanted her with him all the time, and for the first time ever was considering asking a woman to move in with him. His mother would hate the idea, would not be receptive to anyone who wasn't Cassidy, but with time she'd come to the same conclusions he had.

Maybe he'd take Beth to meet his parents the next time they were both off work together and after that, he'd see about asking her to move in with him. Not just to have her in his bed every night but for the waking time he was home, too. He enjoyed her company, enjoyed her sharp wit and fast comebacks, enjoyed how she stimulated his mind as much as she did his body.

Speaking of stimulation, where was she?

"Hey, baby, hurry up and maybe we can get another game of checkers in. Maybe I'll let you win again," he called, getting antsy that he'd been away from her for so long when he knew she was so close.

"I'm game if you are," came her voice from right behind him, "but we both know you didn't let me win, Old Man. I won fair and square. All three games."

Startled that she was behind him, Eli turned. His jaw dropped. He whistled. "Wow."

Striking a pose that was meant to be silly but had his pulse quickening, Beth smiled.

"I've died and gone to heaven."

"Not yet." She batted her eyelashes in mock innocence, just about doing him in. "But you might think so in about twenty minutes."

Eli stood from the recliner, soaked in the lovely vision of her, letting his gaze travel from the upsweep of her hair, several damp tendrils hanging loose, the desire in her made-up eyes, the soft pout to her full lips, the smooth curve of her neck and shoulders, the fullness of her breasts beneath the red lace, the narrowing of her waist and flare of her rounded hips, her shapely legs that looked long in her red stilettos.

He'd never seen her in shoes like these, in anything other than sensible tennis shoes, actually. He whistled again.

"Have I ever mentioned to you that I have a foot fetish?"

She glanced down at her feet, lifting one high heel off the floor as if examining it, then met his gaze. "Really? A foot fetish? Who knew?"

He clicked off the television, dropped the remote, and reached for her. "It's a rather new thing for me but powerful. I think I should show you."

"Actually, I planned to show you."

Eli arched his brow. "Show me?"

She nodded and twirled something he had just noticed in her hand. "Take off your clothes."

Not quite sure where she was going with this but having a pretty good idea, he pulled his shirt over his head, tossed it onto the floor and put himself into Beth's hands, figuratively and literally.

CHAPTER TEN

"HEY, ELI. YOU have a sec?"

"Sure thing." Eli stopped on his way to the ICU and waited for Andrew to catch up with him. A few more minutes before seeing Beth wasn't going to kill him. Maybe. He'd not seen her since he'd dropped her off at her house the night before. It had been late and as much as he hadn't wanted to leave, he'd gone home so they could both get some rest before starting their work week. Every second without her seemed like an eternity. Crazy to think that just a few weeks ago he hadn't known her.

"You headed to ICU?"

Eli nodded. As fast as he could get there. A beautiful brunette he was crazy about was there and he needed to reassure himself that she was real.

"Me, too." Andrew fell into step with him. "So, how's it going?"

Eli wondered if his colleague realized how weird his voice sounded. How weird his question was.

"It's good," he answered, guessing the real reason for Andrew wanting a minute with him. "You?"

"Good." Andrew punched a code into the locked double door that separated the office complex from the private breezeway that led into the hospital. "I took Cassidy out this weekend."

This was good. Very good. "Oh?"

"That okay with you?"

"More than okay. I think it's great," he answered honestly. He wanted Cassidy to be happy, to find someone who could appreciate her the way he appreciated Beth, although he couldn't imagine any man appreciating another woman that much. "She's a wonderful person."

Andrew's expression was pensive. "You haven't changed your mind about getting back together with her, then?"

Eli frowned at his colleague. "Definitely not. We're friends, nothing more."

But rather than look relieved, Andrew sighed. "Guess that rules out that theory."

"What theory is that?"

"She told me that we could only be friends so I figured maybe you were reconsidering."

"We've not discussed how she feels about dating right now so I'm not sure where her head is on that subject. Maybe she just wants to go slow." He hoped that was it, because Andrew was a nice guy who seemed to really care for his friend.

Andrew shrugged. "Maybe. Or maybe she is really in love with you and thinks with time she'll win you back. Knowing her, she will."

Cassidy didn't want him back. Since she'd sexted him, she'd also admitted that perhaps he was right that they'd fallen into their relationship and needed to explore options. She'd asked him what it was that had made him realize she wasn't the perfect woman for him. He hadn't been able to come up with a good answer because he didn't know why he hadn't been able to fall for the perfect woman. Why hadn't he been able to commit to a woman who complemented his life so well?

And what about Beth? He was planning to ask her to move in with him, but if he hadn't been able to commit to Cassidy, what made him think he'd be able to commit to Beth?

"That what you think is going to happen?" Andrew prompted, when Eli became lost in his own thoughts rather than responding.

"I'm sorry that things didn't work out between the two of you," he began, because he really was.

"Me, too, but I'm not going to chase a woman who's in love with another man." Andrew stopped in the hallway, just shy of the ICU nurses' station. "I'm not sure what happened between the two of you, but I just thought you should know that she's still in love with you, because you'd be a fool not to go back to her."

Eli grimaced. Cassidy wasn't any more in love with him than he'd been in love with her. Yes, they did love each other, but not that way. That had been the problem. They hadn't been in love with each other. They hadn't pushed each other's emotions to the limits, not like he and Beth did. Whereas Cassidy had been calm and secure, life had made Beth a flight risk and insecure. And being with her made him question everything he'd once thought he'd wanted. What he and Beth shared was the best relationship he'd ever been in. Also the scariest.

Suddenly she was right in front of him and his heart thudded to a thunderous beat.

She stared directly into his eyes, but the happiness that had shined in their depths had faded to cloudy and unsure and he knew exactly why.

* * *

Wishing she hadn't spotted Eli, hadn't been so excited to see him that she'd immediately headed his way just to say hi, Beth choked back the emotion welling within her. She was not going to overreact as she had the day in Manny's room. Things were good between her and Eli, had been since that day, had been wonderful this past weekend. In many ways her relationship with Eli was perfect.

Except *she* wasn't perfect.

Except she'd just overheard his cardiologist friend advising him to go back to his ex, who was perfect.

And he wasn't saying no. How was she supposed to feel about that?

Beth's stomach churned, threatening to upchuck the grilled chicken salad she'd scarfed down at lunch.

"Hi, Beth," Eli acknowledged her, his eyes begging her not to react to what she'd heard, which stabbed a very vulnerable spot inside her chest.

"How are my patients today?" he continued, as if Beth hadn't heard what Dr. Morgan had just said. Did he think her deaf? Or just dumb?

Why wasn't he telling his friend that he didn't want to go back to Cassidy? That he was happy with his new girlfriend? Why wasn't he taking her into his arms and reassuring her that history was not going to repeat itself?

Sure, they weren't advertising that they were seeing each other outside the hospital, but perhaps more people were catching on to something going on between them than she'd thought because a couple of the other nurses had commented on her seeing more than her fair share of Eli's patients since he'd become single. Another had commented on how she must have had one heck of a weekend because she practically glowed this morning.

She wasn't glowing now. She was trying to not want to strangle him for refusing to acknowledge that she had a place in his life, outside the hospital. Why wasn't he? For that matter, why hadn't she let on to anyone at the hospital that she and Eli were an item? Was she afraid of jinxing their relationship by telling someone? Or was she trying to save face for if/when he realized Cassidy was the woman for him and he went back to her?

"Sorry, Dr. Randolph." She emphasized his formal name. "I didn't mean to interrupt you and Dr. Morgan."

"Not a problem. Andrew and I were finished, I

believe?" He looked at the other man for confirmation then back at Beth. She could see the concern in his eyes, knew he knew she wasn't happy. Surely he didn't have to question what about.

"Oh, yeah, sure thing," Dr. Morgan told him, not even looking at Beth but focusing on Eli. "Good luck and I hope you realize what a lucky man you are to have Cassidy waiting in the wings when you get your act together."

To give him credit, Eli winced.

Beth hoped she hadn't, but suspected that if all she had done was wince she'd consider trying out for Emily's next theatrical production. In reality, she felt as if the cardiologist had delivered a blow to her chest.

Was that what Eli was doing?

What would she do if Eli left her? Losing Barry to his ex had hurt and she'd never felt about him the way she felt about Eli. How would she recover from such a loss?

"Excuse me," she managed despite the spasms rocking her chest, despite the moisture stinging her eyes. Without another glance, she left the two men near the nurses' station. She went into a patient room, grateful her patient was asleep, and checked telemetry. Anything to be doing some-thing with her shaky hands.

Could she recover if Eli left her? Sure, she'd go through life's motions, but would her heart ever be whole again?

"Beth?"

She turned, gave him a weak smile. "Hi."

"Hi," he said back, looking relieved and a bit cautious. What had he expected? For her to spear him with an IV pole? "I'm sorry you had to hear that."

"Because it's true?" she asked, amazed at how calm her voice sounded when her insides shook.

"Cassidy isn't waiting for me. She and I are fin-ished as more than friends. I've told you that."

He had told her. Several times. Granted, she had heard that before, but she couldn't judge Eli by Barry's sins. Yet history did have a tendency to repeat itself. She fought to keep walls from going up, but she felt so vulnerable that doing so was difficult.

"Why didn't it work with Cassidy? She seems so perfect. What if you realize that someday?"

He shrugged. "I don't know and Cassidy is as close to perfect as they come. I already know that and I don't want her. I want you." He glanced toward the sleeping patient, ran his fingers through his hair. "This is a conversation we should save for later, don't you think?"

He was right, of course. They were at work.

"That's fine."

"Which is what my mother used to always say to my father when he'd upset her and she refused to talk about it, but would make him pay dearly for it later."

She lifted her gaze to his, her breath catching as it always did when she looked at him, amazed that even for a brief period of time he wanted her.

"I'm not refusing to talk," she clarified. "I do think we need to talk about this."

Studying her, he nodded. "You're right. Good. We'll talk tonight."

"As for the other, I've never made you pay for anything. I've given you all I have to give and not asked for anything in return."

Eli's face contorted with confusion. "What is that supposed to mean?"

She glanced at their patient, who was still breathing evenly via the oxygen nasal cannula. "Like you said, we'll talk later."

* * *

Punching in her code to get into the medicine cart, Beth tried not to stare at the ethereal beauty of the blonde woman chatting with a resident a few yards away from the nurses' station. Cassidy smiled, touched her upswept hair, and pointed out something on the computer tablet the resident was showing her.

Was she waiting for Eli? It made sense. That they'd been together for so long, that he'd want one last wild ride prior to settling down for the rest of his life. It's what men did, right?

Emily waved her hand in front of Beth's face. "Hello. Anybody home in there?"

Absently, Beth nodded. Emily didn't routinely work in the ICU, but her friend was picking up an extra shift to cover for Leah, who was missing more work than attending these days.

"Um, am I imagining things or are you not smiling any more? Is everything okay with Dr. Do Me All Night? Or should I say Dr. Do You All Night?" Emily teased, nudging Beth's arm to try to get her to smile. When Beth didn't, Emily moved in front of her, blocking her view of Eli's ex. "Okay, tell me what's up before you stare a hole in Dr. Qualls's head. This morning you were walking on clouds, telling me you'd had the best weekend of your life, showing me goofy pictures of you and Dr. Wild Wild West, now you look on the verge of crying… or murdering someone."

"She wants him back," Beth mused, imagining the scenario. Maybe when they talked tonight he'd tell her as much, that ultimately he'd go back to Cassidy, that she, Beth, was good enough for a weekend romp but long term he'd chose to go back to the good doctor.

"So what? What sane woman wouldn't want him back?" Emily countered, as if Beth hadn't just told her something earth-shattering. Any moment Beth expected her to fake a yawn.

Eyes suddenly stinging, Beth felt rising panic in her throat, panic she couldn't control. "He thinks she's perfect and he's going to go back to her."

Emily frowned. "Has he told you that? After spending all weekend with you, he told you that he thinks she's perfect and he's going to go back to her? When? This morning?"

"He did say she was perfect, but he hasn't said he was going to go back to her. But I know he's going to."

Pinching the bridge of her nose, Emily shook her head. "Why would he do that when you two are getting along so fabulously? And why did he tell you she was perfect?"

Beth gestured in the direction where Cassidy stood with the resident. "I'm not her and I said she was perfect and he agreed with me."

Emily shook her head. "Thank goodness, and why would you say she was perfect? Obviously she isn't perfect for Eli."

Confused, Beth blinked at her friend.

"She had her chance and things didn't work out. You're the woman in his life now. Be grateful and quit looking for problems that aren't there. You are in his life and I'm grateful for that. I want you happy and have been worried that it's taken you so long to date someone else."

"Eli and I aren't really dating. We have sex together, but that's it. You know that." Beth closed the medicine cart and electronically signed off that she'd removed her patient's next medication dosage.

"You went away with him for the weekend, you have sex with him, call it what you will, but you are dating the man." Emily logged into the computerized medication cart and removed the medication for her patient as well. She closed the drawer, electronically signed that she had removed the medication, then gave Beth a thoughtful look. "You're happier than I've ever known you to be and at the same time you're scared to believe in that happiness because you don't have any real faith in his feelings for you. What does Eli say when you ask him to define your relationship?"

"He doesn't say anything because I don't ask him."

Emily rolled her eyes. "Beth, you have told the man your every fantasy. You've experienced quite a few of those fantasies with him. You just spend the entire weekend with him. Surely you can ask him to define the terms of your relationship."

"But…"

But she didn't feel as if she could. Which was ridiculous.

Emily was right. If she could get naked with the man, she should be able to carry on a conversation with him.

Actually, she could. After they'd had sex they'd had brilliant conversations. This weekend they'd had brilliant conversations about so many things.

About everything but what was happening between them.

Well, that wasn't exactly true. They did talk about sex.

About how in tune their bodies were. About how each time they were together they brought the other higher and higher. Physically they seemed to be able to discuss anything, their wants, desires, needs, what pleased them most. How they talked to each other, how comfortable she felt telling him where she wanted to be touched and how amazed Beth, but when she was with him she felt completely in sync with him, completely comfortable. Unless she let her brain start working.

Once that pesky organ kicked in, she questioned her bliss.

After all, if Eli had any real intentions toward her, even of dating her, he'd have taken her to dinner rather than feeding her at her house each night. He'd have wanted the world to know that they were dating, that she was no longer available, because, hello, with the way it was that guy from Administration had still been asking her out even. She had gently told him no, not interested, but if people actually knew she and Eli were an item she wouldn't have had to do anything. Every man would have known they didn't stand a chance when compared to Eli. Dr. Morgan wouldn't have been telling Eli to go back to his ex in front of her.

But, for whatever reason, Eli was content with the status quo.

Pure and simple, he wanted sex from her. No strings attached.

She wanted sex from him, too. Had initially believed that anything with Eli was so much more than she'd ever believed even a possibility and she'd be content with whatever he'd give her.

Only she wasn't. She wanted more. Was that why she hadn't made a big deal of their relationship at work? Because she wanted more, knew ultimately he didn't, and as long as no one else knew, she wouldn't have to see their pitying looks when things ended? There was only one way she could think of to protect herself.

"Uh-oh. I'm not liking that expression."

Beth took a deep breath and gave her best friend a tight smile. "I can't see Eli any more."

Emily's eyes widened, but her friend only waited for her to say more.

"But I may not be able to not see him."

"What's that supposed to mean? If seeing Cassidy is what triggered this current line of thought, you're being ridiculous. This is your Barry hang-ups coming to surface. Eli is not Barry. You need to talk to him, tell him how you feel."

Yes, she supposed she did. That she would. Tonight. When they talked.

Eli pulled off his scrub mask and cap, left the operating room, and headed straight for the ICU.

He'd been tied up in the OR all afternoon, doing bronchoscopies, and he'd not seen Beth since she'd overheard Andrew talking about Cassidy and their exchange in the sleeping patient's room. He was finished with work for the day but wanted to see Beth before leaving the hospital. He'd do so under the guise of checking on a patient but, really, he just needed to see her. There had been a worrisome light in her eyes that concerned him, made him wonder what was going on in that sharp brain of hers.

He hadn't known quite what to expect when he'd seen her standing there, watched her expression transform from one of happiness to uncertainty.

He'd watched her walls go up, had felt himself being shut out.

They did need to talk. Tonight.

He needed to explain about Cassidy. Only how did he explain what he didn't really understand himself? Everything with Cassidy had been so easy and that hadn't worked. Everything with Beth felt so out of control, so intense. What was it about easy that hadn't worked for him that he'd choose this craziness of needing Beth so much?

He paused, took a deep breath. Quite frankly, his choices didn't make logical sense.

"Code Blue, Room 312," he heard someone call down the ICU hallway, then realized it was Beth.

He was almost there, but took off at a jog as Beth rushed a crash cart into the patient room. Just as he entered the room, another nurse followed him inside to record the code.

He paused only a millisecond when he saw who else was in the room. Cassidy leaned over the bed, compressing the patient's chest.

Beth opened the crash cart, gave an injection of epinephrine at Cassidy's order, then prepared the defibrillator.

"Here, let me." Eli took over for Cassidy on the

compressions, because he well knew how exhausting doing CPR on a person was. Until one had actually performed the procedure it was difficult to comprehend just how much effort was required. "You do the air bag."

"Thank God, it's you!" Cassidy exclaimed, stepping up to the head of the bed and squeezing the air bag to deliver another breath to the flatlined patient. Eli recognized the older lady as one he'd seen a couple of times after she'd been transferred to a local nursing facility and Cassidy had requested he consult on her care.

Eli shot her a reassuring look and focused on compressing the woman's chest while Beth put on the defibrillator pads. Beth hadn't acknowledged his presence in the room at all, had just stayed safely tucked behind those walls she'd erected earlier.

"Ready?" he asked her, not liking being completely ignored regardless of the situation.

Not looking his way, Beth nodded and called, "All clear."

Eli and Cassidy stepped back from the patient and Beth pressed the button that would deliver the jolt of electricity to the patient's heart. Nothing. No heartbeat. No gasp of breath.

Eli started compressions again while the defibrillator reset itself.

Cassidy gave a squeeze to deliver air. "We have to save her, Eli. She's such a sweet little lady."

"I know." He gave her a look of commiseration. Cassidy always took losing a patient hard, always felt that she was somehow responsible, when, regardless of anything any medical professional did, eventually nature was always going to take its course.

Her compassion for her patients was one of the things that made Cassidy such a good doctor but was also one of the reasons why she stressed so much and gave so much of herself to medicine. Maybe that's why they'd never had any sparks. Because Cassidy's real passion was medicine and he'd only been in her life because he fit so well into that.

Staying in rhythm with his compressions, he shot a glance her way, admired the doctor she was, the woman she was, and understood how he'd been in a relationship with her for so long, understood how he'd wanted his relationship with her to be more than it had been.

But he also knew he'd never settle for what they'd had. Not ever again.

Beth focused on what she did, on getting the defibrillator reset to deliver another shock to their patient, but she wasn't blind. Or deaf. She'd have had to be to miss the emotions between Eli and Cassidy. Perhaps Dr. Morgan had been right. Perhaps Cassidy was waiting for Eli to sew his wild oats and return to her to settle down.

Perhaps that's exactly what he was doing.

She was the wild oats he was sewing.

She glanced toward him, seeking some reassurance that she wasn't, but caught him staring at Cassidy with something akin to awe.

Another one of those blows to her chest hit, but she forced herself to focus on their patient. A woman was dying, was technically already dead. They all needed to focus. Their patient took precedence over Eli Randolph and his perfect blonde beauty.

"There's no one I'd rather have at my side during a code," Cassidy said to Eli.

La-la-la, Beth chanted in her head, not wanting to eavesdrop on this particular conversation. Not wanting to be in this room. Why had she had to choose nursing as a profession? Surely she could have done something less demanding? Something less likely to put her in a room with the man she was crazy about working alongside his ex-girl-friend?

"You remember that code we worked together during residency at Vanderbilt?"

Beth's ears must have heard her thought because her brain couldn't interpret Eli's muffled reply. Good, she didn't want to know if he remembered spending time during residency with the woman beside him. It was bad enough that she'd had to see that look, that admiration and emotion on his face when he'd looked at his ex.

"All clear," she called, grateful the machine had reset. It seemed to take forever, when actually only a few seconds had passed.

Eli and Cassidy stepped clear of the patient. The woman's body gave a jerk, then nothing. No breath. No pulse. No anything.

They continued to work on the patient, trying to revive the woman, but to no avail. Finally, when all hope was gone and had been for some time, Eli called the code.

"No, Eli, don't do it," Cassidy pleaded, squeezing the air bag to deliver another breath to affirm her position. Her big blue eyes implored him to not stop. "We have to keep trying. For her family's sake."

"She's gone, Cass. There's nothing we can do." His voice was gentle, full of comfort.

His use of the shortened name jolted Beth's heart as surely as the defibrillator had shaken their patient.

Losing a patient always hit Beth hard. She'd only worked a few codes, all of which had left her in emotional turmoil. Currently, she wasn't sure if it was the code or the couple making her feel as if her legs might give out from beneath her.

Once Eli called the code, the intensity in the room faded. All except the intensity of the emotions twirling through Beth's brain and that clung to the air so heavily it weighed her down to where even moving felt impossible.

The recorder placed her hand on Cassidy's arm. "I'm sorry, Dr. Qualls. You did everything you could. You and Dr. Randolph make a good team."

Hello, Beth thought. What was she? Chopped liver? She'd been a part of the code team too. Was she totally invisible or what?

But the recorder was right.

Looking at Eli, how perfectly handsome he was,

and at the watery-eyed beauty next to him, Beth had to admit they made a great couple.

They looked so perfect together, so yin and yang. Eli might believe he wouldn't go back to Cassidy, but how could he not go back to her?

"Sorry," Cassidy sniffed, wiping at her face with the side of her hand. "I'm being silly, aren't I?"

Eli gave her a compassionate smile. "I've always said you had too big a heart."

"Yeah, you have always said that." Cassidy's gaze lifted to his and she gave a weak self-derisive smile. "Better hope I don't decide to take up drinking again tonight. You might get another crazy text."

Eli shot a nervous glance toward where Beth was restoring the crash cart. Her job. That's all she was doing. Nothing more. She wasn't eavesdropping. She wasn't feeling like a fifth wheel. She wasn't wondering what kind of crazy text Cassidy had sent him.

"Oops, sorry, Beth," Cassidy apologized, following Eli's gaze. "I forgot you were in here."

Beth didn't say anything. What could she say? Apparently she was chopped liver, totally invisible, and all too quickly forgotten. Or maybe chopped liver wasn't right. Maybe wild oats was a more apt description.

"This guy has a way of making a woman forget a lot of things." Cassidy patted his biceps. "Will you go with me to talk to the family? I could use the moral support."

Beth bit the inside of her lip. Awkward—that's all she could think. This situation was totally awkward and she just wanted out of there.

"You know I will," Eli told her, then his gaze met Beth's and what she saw scared her. His expression was guarded, as if he didn't want her to know his thoughts, his emotions.

If she wasn't careful she was going to have her heart broken.

Beth had sworn that she and Eli were going to talk and not have sex when he arrived at her house that night. So how was it that their food sat untouched somewhere between her front door and her bedroom and they lay naked, breathing hard, in her bed?

Was she just feeling desperate for one last time, one last touch, one last memory because she knew what she had to do? That she needed to walk away before he did?

Lying in his arms, she traced her fingertips over Eli's chest, liking the smoothness of his skin, the slight roughness of hair that grew there, the muscles that rippled just beneath the surface of his skin. Quite simply, she liked everything about him and was addicted to him as surely as if she were a druggie. He was her high, always leaving her needing one more fix, one more kiss, one more touch.

Maybe Emily was right and she just needed to talk to tell him what was running through her mind. Maybe her past hang-ups really did play tricks on her and she was angsting for nothing. Maybe. Maybe not.

Because although Eli had acted just as desperate for her physically, he had been distracted from the moment he'd walked into her house.

"What are we?" She couldn't believe the question had slipped out of her mouth quite so easily.

"We are pretty spectacular." As if to prove his point, he bent and kissed the bend of her elbow, then blew hot breath onto the slightly moist skin.

Her goose-bumps got goose-bumps. But she wasn't going to be sidetracked. Something was definitely on his mind other than her tonight and earlier he'd been all googly-eyed over his ex-girlfriend right after his friend had been encouraging him to go back to her. Was he thinking himself a fool for being with the wrong woman?

"Sexually, yes, we are." She couldn't deny how spectacular they were. "But what are we beyond sex?"

"What do you mean, what are we beyond sex?" He looked genuinely confused. "Don't you know?"

Beth sat up in her bed, fluffed her pillow behind her back and met his gaze head on. "Actually, I don't, but I'd like you to tell me, please, because I'd like to." She hesitated, pulled the covers up over her body, suddenly not wanting him to see her body, not wanting to feel vulnerable to him.

Unfortunately, the sheets were so tangled at their feet that she barely covered her legs, much less anything vital, and, really, her body wasn't what was most vulnerable to the man studying her.

Giving up on the sheets, she crossed her arms over her bare breasts, because, really, how seriously could he take her when her nipples were still all quivery from his touch? "Am I your wild oats?"

"What? Where did that come from?" Eyes wide,

he sat up and went from looking semi-amused to shocked.

"You heard me."

"Of course you're not."

"Then what am I?"

"I've told you what you are."

Beth frowned. "When have you told me what I am? Because I pay close attention to every word that leaves your mouth, to everything you do. I don't recall you ever telling me what I am to you."

"Then you've not been paying close enough attention, Beth." He took her hand into his, lifted it to his mouth and pressed a kiss to her palm. "You're mine."

Involuntarily, she shivered then jerked her hand free, because right now was not the time to be reacting physically.

"You're the woman I wake up thinking about, that I think about all day long, that I go to sleep thinking about." He laced their fingers, held her hand firmly within his. "You, Beth. No one else."

She couldn't help herself. "Not Cassidy?" Beth felt his flinch and the effect was like a bucket of ice water dumped over the warmth of his previous words.

"I don't think of Cassidy when you and I are to-gether. Surely you don't believe I could think of anyone but you when we are together?"

When they were together. Was there significance in his repeating that?

"But you do think about her?"

"Yes," he admitted, and Beth's breath gushed from her lungs in a painful whoosh. "But not like you're obviously taking my answer."

"How am I supposed to take your answer when you say that sometimes you think about your ex-girlfriend?"

His jaw worked back and forth as if he was agi-tated. "The way it was intended."

"Which was?"

"You asked me if I ever think about Cassidy. She was the most important person in my life for the past few years," he pointed out, sounding way too logical. "Of course I think about her. I care about her."

He wasn't denying his feelings for his ex the way Barry had. Eli was flat out admitting that he still cared for Cassidy. Great. She scrambled to get out of the bed. "Maybe you should be in her bed and not in mine."

He grabbed her just as she was standing, wrapped his arms around her waist and pulled her back down to the bed. She scuffled with him, but only half-heartedly because she didn't want to walk away from him. Not really. She also didn't want him to see the tears forming in her eyes so she closed them.

With care not to hurt her, he pushed her back onto the bed, covered her with his body to where Beth couldn't have gone anywhere had she really wanted to.

When long moments passed without him saying anything more, she opened her eyes, met his gaze. His very blue, very intense gaze that was staring straight into her soul, or so it sure seemed.

"You're not paying close enough attention again."

Beth swallowed, knowing he was going to continue without her having to say more.

"Cassidy was the most important person, as in past tense."

Hope welled in Beth's stomach, but she'd been down this road before, had walked that mile, and suffered the road rash to her heart before the kill had come.

Why stick around for the axe to fall?

"She isn't any more. Right now, in the present tense, you are the most important person in my life, Beth. You."

Oh, sweetness. She wanted to believe him, to believe in him, but her doubts ran deep. She'd been burned before and knew better than to play with fire. Eli was fire. "Because of sex?"

He gave a light snort. "Sex with you is amazing, but I think there's more to you and me than just sex. Don't you feel the connection between us?"

Beth closed her eyes, unable to take the intensity of his gaze a moment longer.

"Tell me you feel this." He put her hand on his chest.

His heart beat strongly against her palm. She bit the inside of her lip. Prayed for strength. She opened her eyes and glared. "You're saying all the right things, but the reality is that you're not doing any of the right things."

That seemed to throw him. "I didn't hear you complaining earlier that I wasn't doing the right things."

Of course he'd misunderstood her. She pushed against his chest and he let her dislodge him, rolling to beside her in the bed. Propping the pillow behind his back, he sat up and raked his fingers through his hair.

She scooted up in the bed, too, because she didn't like him towering over her. "Say what you will, but I saw you with Dr. Qualls today."

His brows veed. He raked his fingers through his hair again and shook his head. "This lack of trust in me is really starting to get old."

His voice sounded angry, offended.

"If you're getting back together with your ex-girlfriend I have a right to know."

He took a deep breath then exhaled slowly. When his gaze met hers his eyes were cold, colder than she'd ever seen or thought possible. "If I was getting back together with my ex-girlfriend, I wouldn't be here. You think I'd be in bed with you while considering getting back together with another woman? You really think that little of me?"

He made it sound impossible, but she knew better. Men did get back together with women from their past. Men lied. To her. She knew that first hand. Hadn't she and Barry had a similar conversation once? Near the end? Right before he'd dumped her to go back to his ex? Right after he'd slept with his ex in the bed he'd shared with *her*? Hadn't he accused her of being crazy? That, of course, he still cared about his ex because of their history together, that he wanted them to still be friends, but that he loved Beth now, and she needed to quit overreacting?

Yes, she'd heard all this before.

Except that Eli hadn't professed words of love. Not that those words had mattered to Barry. They hadn't. Wouldn't it be better to end everything now rather than live in constant fear of him leaving?

"Obviously you don't believe anything I say, because I have repeatedly told you that I'm not getting back together with Cassidy."

She wanted to believe him. She wanted to trust that he wouldn't break her heart.

She wanted him to be in love with her and no one else.

Oh, God. She wanted him to be in love with her.

She took a deep breath, met his gaze, and went on the offensive. "What am I supposed to think when you looked so torn when you were looking at her?"

What indeed? Eli wondered, trying to squelch his anger that Beth would think so little of him. "Let's just set the story straight here one last time and I do mean one last time because I am not going to keep rehashing this." He gave her a pointed look. "I'm not getting back together with Cassidy. Ever."

Leaning back against the bed's headboard, Beth seemed to be digesting his words. She closed her eyes, took another deep breath as if she fought hyperventilating and asked, "Do you love her, Eli?"

"Sure I do."

Beth's gasp warned he'd said the wrong thing. Her rapid scoot away from him confirmed his bad move. He was trying to be honest, to tell her everything, but she was as prickly as a porcupine and words were failing him.

"Beth." He grabbed her wrist, pulled her back when she tried to scramble off the bed. "Let me elaborate. I love her, but I am not nor have I ever been in love with Cassidy. I wanted to be, but it just never happened."

"I don't understand." Which was clear by the lost look on her face. "You wanted to be in love with her?"

"Sure I did. She's a wonderful woman who fits perfectly with what I want in a woman and wife someday."

"Oh." She didn't sound thrilled with his explanation, and with the way he was fumbling around with words he couldn't blame her.

"At least I thought she was. I was wrong. We didn't have a physical connection."

"Oh," she repeated, not sounding any happier with his clarification. "I guess that's where I come in."

Eli sighed in frustration. "We're more than just a physical connection, Beth. You know that."

If she did, she ignored him, focusing on his previous comment instead. "If Dr. Qualls fits perfectly what you want in a woman and wife, what does that make me exactly? I'm not sure how to label our relationship."

"You want me to label us?" He scratched his head. Hadn't he been asking himself exactly what Beth was to him since the night they'd first made love? She amazed him, stole his breath, left him wanting more and more. Quite simply, he couldn't get enough of her.

"First, let me clarify, that I thought Cassidy was the perfect woman for me once upon a time, that on paper I guess she still is, but in reality…"

Beth sat stiffly next to him, staring straight ahead as if afraid to even look at him. "In reality?"

If their conversation wasn't so serious, Eli might laugh at how haughty her expression was, at how she held her body so rigid. When she'd questioned him about Cassidy, he'd gotten just as prickly as she was. He wanted Beth to believe in him unconditionally, and it irked that she had so little faith in him. But none of that changed the truth.

"In reality, she isn't you."

Beth swallowed again, still didn't look at him. "And that matters because?"

"I want you."

"Yes, I know. We have physical sparks." She made her words sound like something dirty. "So you want me until the attraction burns out?"

He supposed, in some ways, what she said was true. That he did want her until the attraction burned out, but he couldn't imagine a time of not wanting her. Not when every touch just left him longing to touch her again, when holding her left him wanting to hold her even closer.

"What if the attraction doesn't wear itself out, Beth? What if it never burns out?"

"Physical attraction always does." She sucked in a deep breath, scooted further away from him, and reached for the tangled sheet at their feet. "So I'm your sex partner until you tire of me?"

Stinging at her confidence that their chemistry would fizzle out, he shrugged. "Or until you tire of me."

Which felt like a much more likely scenario because he couldn't fathom ever getting his fill of her. Yet she seemed convinced that they were doomed from the start.

"So our relationship is solely about sex?"

"You know that isn't true."

"How do I know that? No one at the hospital even knows we've been seeing each other."

"What is it you'd have me to do? Have a T-shirt printed proclaiming that I can't get enough of you? Perhaps I should have two printed so you can wear one as well?"

She glanced at him with narrowed eyes. "Don't be a smart aleck."

"Don't not believe me when I tell you I'm not your ex."

"Don't expect me to believe you when I saw how you looked at your ex, at how perfect you two were together." She took a deep breath and looked him straight in the eyes. "Plus, what did she mean when she said that about drinking and sending you a crazy text?"

There it was. What Eli had been struggling with from the moment Cassidy had mentioned it. He needed to set the story straight with Beth. He needed to tell her the truth about the night he'd first texted her. All evening that thought had distracted him.

"She drank more than she should have and she texted me," he began.

Beth's lips twisted. "What did she text you?"

Eli winced. He hated this, felt as if he was betraying Cassidy by telling what had happened, but making things right with Beth was more important. "She sent me a sext."

Beth gasped. "When?"

"The night I first texted you."

"The night…" Beth's eyes widened, filled with confusion. "Cassidy sexted you and you sexted me?"

"Something like that." Part of him said to leave it at that, not to elaborate, but he didn't want secrets between him and Beth. "I took the photo to send to her."

Beth's lips parted, she shook her head and

she scooted away from him, partially hanging off the bed.

"I didn't send it to her, Beth. I was erasing her number and hit another number and send by accident."

"My text was an accident? You hit my number and sent to me by mistake?"

Oh, yeah, Beth was a flight risk and she was ready to take off any moment.

"Your text was the best thing that's ever happened to me."

"I can't believe this. From the beginning, it's all been a lie."

"Nothing has been a lie, Beth."

"Sure it has. You never even meant to text me. I'm a mistake."

He couldn't deny it. "I was a fool not to have noticed you before our texting."

"This is all just sexual."

"It's not."

"Then what is it, Eli? Because that's sure what it feels like from where I'm sitting," she accused. "You're using me for one last fling before settling into your perfect happily-ever-after. Great, y'all go be perfect together."

"I'm not and that's not what I want."

"Right." Her word dripped with acid. "I'm not stupid."

Eli raked his fingers through his hair. "If you really don't believe me, if you really believe she and I are perfect together, then I should leave." He wasn't sure where the claim came from, but when Beth just shrugged her shoulders as if it didn't matter one way or the other if he stayed or went, Eli reached for his pants.

"Go ahead and leave. It's what you're destined to do. Maybe you could sext her on your way home."

"You really should get that chip off your shoulder, Beth. Until you do, you aren't going to trust anyone and that lack of trust is going to make you one lonely woman."

"Ha," she scoffed, covering herself completely with the sheet. "Blame it on me that you're leaving. We both know it was only a matter of time before you went back to Cassidy. I'm just an accident."

Eli put on his shoes and looked around the room. His shirt must be somewhere on the way to the front door. Good. That's where he was headed.

When he reached her bedroom door, he paused.

"You're not an accident, Beth. You were fate. My fate. I'm in love with you, but without trust there's really not a reason for me to stay."

The walls shrouding her didn't budge. "I didn't hear anyone ask you to stay."

Wincing, Eli turned, walked away from Beth and didn't look back. Time enough for regrets later.

"He said what?" Emily screeched, smacking her forehead like she could have had a V8.

"You heard me." Because Beth wasn't repeating herself. Not again. She'd been repeating herself over and over in her head and she didn't want to hear the words again. Not in her head. Not in her heart. Certainly, not out loud.

"You need to tell him you're sorry. Beg him to forgive you. Whatever you have to do, just make things right with him."

Beth stared at her best friend, not sure she'd heard her correctly. "Huh?"

"You single-handedly chopped your relationship with Eli to smithereens because you were too scared to believe in it." Emily slapped her hands against the tabletop. "Fix it."

"No."

Emily's drawn-on brows veed deeply. "Why not?"

"Because some things can't be fixed."

"Some things can. Fix this. Before it's too late, make this right."

"What are you so concerned about? There are more men in the sea."

"Seriously?" Emily shook her head with disappointment. "You're sure about that? Because I'm pretty sure where you are concerned, there aren't."

Beth winced. "Don't say that."

"What? That you had your fantasy guy eating out of your hand, literally I might add, and you blew it. He told you he loved you and you shot him down."

Wincing, Beth crossed her arms. "Why are you taking his side?"

"Because he's right. You are so paranoid that he's going to do the same thing Barry did that you pushed him away."

"Hello, it's not as if we've been seeing each other that long. Just a couple of weeks. How could he have loved me? Besides, ultimately, he did do what Barry did, didn't he?"

Gossip had it that Eli and Cassidy were together again. That their working the code together must have ignited old feelings, because they'd been seen together repeatedly. Just like ole times, Beth had overheard one nurse say.

Gag. Just three days after he'd walked out of Beth's house he was already back together with Cassidy. So much for his claims of love.

"Yeah, after you giftwrapped him and sent him back to her. Beth, you've got to deal with what Barry did, let it go, and move on with your life without the past shadowing the present and future. Now. Fix this while there is still hope because of course Eli could really love you. Time doesn't dictate emotion. Love happens. Sometimes immediately. Sometimes gradually." Emily rolled her eyes with great frustration. "How you couldn't realize that when you're madly in love with the man yourself is beyond me."

"I'm not in love with him."

Emily snorted. "Sure you're not."

"I'm not. I…" Beth hesitated, her words tearing at her heart, but she forced them out all the same. "He was my fantasy guy, Emily. Nothing more."

"Keep telling yourself that if you need to, but I'm not buying it and neither is your heart."

* * *

Beth lay in bed, thinking over her conversation with Emily. Had she pushed Eli into Cassidy's arms? Probably. Definitely.

Lord, she missed him.

With the clarity of hindsight she knew pride had gotten in her way, as had the past and fear.

She hadn't wanted him to leave. She'd wanted to beg him to stay, to love her, to stay forever, to somehow convince her that she was the one for him. But she hadn't said any of those things.

Because she hadn't trusted him to stay.

Because she hadn't believed in his feelings for her.

Because she'd known he was going to go back to Cassidy so she'd not let him behind her walls.

Only he had gotten behind her walls all the same.

Her insides ached without him.

Her heart ached without him.

Because she loved him.

He'd said he loved her. She'd let him leave, practically forced him to.

Idiot! she told herself. How could she have just let him walk way when in doing so he'd carried her heart with him?

She picked up her phone, opened it, clicked on the text message icon. She took a deep breath then clicked the screen off button. What could she say? That she'd changed her mind? That she wanted him back? That she loved him and needed him and was lost without him?

Would he believe her?

No, probably not. She needed to show him. To show him those things. To prove to him that she trusted him.

But how?

She knew, of course. The answer was obvious and one she'd sworn she'd never do.

Love made one do a lot of things one thought one would never do.

Like don a naughty red nightie and take a risqué selfie.

Eli smiled weakly at the woman sitting across the restaurant table from him.

"I'll make a deal with you," she offered. "I'll agree to go out with Andrew again if you will call Beth."

"Wouldn't do any good."

"You think she'd say no? It's obvious she misses

you. I see how she looks at you at the hospital, how she looks at me. She's crazy about you and hates me with a passion."

Eli had done his best to avoid seeing Beth. Not an easy feat since Nurse Rogers was still assigning his patients to Beth. Fortunately, Beth had a lot of past experience in avoiding him and their paths had barely crossed. "She might say yes, but it doesn't matter. She doesn't trust me and we'd just end up right back at this same place."

He and Cassidy had talked so much the past few days. He'd needed his friend after leaving Beth's house, had gone to her and spilt the truth about everything. She'd listened, scolded him for not being straightforward with her from the beginning, and then told him he needed to win Beth back because he was obviously in love with her.

He loved Beth.

But love without trust was useless.

He wanted what his parents had, what he'd believed he could have with Beth, but she was so scarred from her relationship with Barry that she didn't know how to trust. No relationship could survive without it.

So he needed to teach her how to trust.

Because he was miserable without her.

But how? How did one teach trust? Wasn't it either one of those things that was inherently there or not there?

"You're doing it again," Cassidy pointed out, taking a sip of her wine.

"What's that?"

"Thinking about her."

"I'm always thinking about her."

"So call her."

"I can't. It's going to take more than a call to convince her to let me inside those walls around her heart."

"Then give her more. Woo her. Earn her trust. If she's the woman for you, prove it to her."

Eli stared at his ex-girlfriend then shrugged. "She is the woman for me. I just don't know how to convince her of that."

Cassidy took a sip of her wine then shrugged. "I'd say that's pretty obvious. Earn her trust, Eli."

It hadn't been a good morning in the ICU. A patient had died just before shift change and that had set the tone for the day. Leah had called in sick again and Nurse Rogers hadn't found a replacement. Beth and the other nurses there had pulled heavier than normal loads, but had made it work. Fortunately they'd had a couple of transfers to a step-down unit and things had almost eerily calmed down in the ICU. Beth only had about another thirty minutes left before her shift change and she was ready to call it a day.

Only she wasn't.

Because she'd not done what she'd toyed with doing the previous night and all day. Her phone burned a hole in her pocket even now, reminding her that she'd not sent her peace offering to Eli. Peace offering? No, her message was more a token of trust.

She had the message typed, had the photo attached. All she had to do was hit send and it would leave her phone. But she'd hesitated. What if she'd waited too long, what if she'd pushed him too far away? What if he was happily back with Cassidy? What if he laughed at her message?

Beth finished checking her comatose patient, logged in the information, then paused in the doorway.

Sending a photo of herself was a scary prospect under any circumstances, was risking making a fool of herself, but to send it when she wasn't even seeing the guy any more? That was pure craziness, right? Or a show of the utmost trust in him that she knew he'd never intentionally hurt her, that she knew her photo was safe in his care, that, although she was scared and had messed up, ultimately she did trust him and he just needed to be patient with her because having a man in her life worthy of trust was all new to her.

Love came with risks. But to shove love away for fear of those risks was just stupid and that's what she'd done.

She'd had something special with Eli and she'd ruined the most precious thing she'd even known. She might not be able to save their relationship, might be a fool for what she was about to do, but she was going to take action all the same.

Because she loved Eli and would fight for him.

She would show him that, despite her fears, she did trust him.

Beth hit send and held her breath as her first real sext photo left her phone.

No turning back now.

Eli would know that her photo wasn't meant to be sexual, although it was. He'd know that it was her showing him she trusted him, that she'd give him that power over her heart, and she trusted him to wield that power with gentle hands and a protective spirit.

She'd thrown out her token of trust. The rest was up to him.

Now she'd wait.

Hopefully, not for the rest of her life.

She left the patient room, headed for the nurses' station, paused at what she saw.

Eli stood in the midst of several nurses and even a couple of doctors. It was an odd sight this late in the evening. Cassidy stood near Eli, laughing at something he'd said.

Had she really just sent a naughty photo of herself to him while he stood in the midst of her coworkers? Seriously? Could her timing have been any worse?

Beth's heart squeezed. Part of her felt like running, but she wouldn't.

Not ever again.

She wouldn't run from love.

Instead, she'd embrace it. Or even chase after it if need be.

She loved Eli and, despite how foolish she'd been,

she wasn't going to let him make the mistake of ending up with the wrong woman for the rest of his life.

Cassidy might be perfect, but she wasn't perfect for Eli.

She was the perfect woman for him.

Neither Cassidy nor any other woman could love him the way that she did. How could she have been so foolish not to have realized that?

Beth almost stumbled when Cassidy noticed her and nudged Eli's shoulder, causing him to turn, face her.

Beth's feet quit working and she paused in mid-step, stopping about ten feet from him.

Everyone around him stepped back as Eli stepped forward. "Beth Taylor, there's something I need to say to you."

Oh, Lord, had he been standing around everyone and opened her text? Had everyone seen her vulnerable photo and that's why they all stared at her as if they knew something she didn't?

She couldn't believe he'd do that. She didn't believe he'd done that. Even if he no longer felt the same about her, he wouldn't have shared her photo. That wasn't who he was. She knew that about him.

Warmth spread through her, knocking down the remaining walls around her heart. She trusted Eli. With her heart, her body, her life.

She stood, head high, shoulders straight, and didn't waver from looking into his blue eyes. She loved him, would do whatever it took to prove that to him, to prove to him that although she'd made mistakes, she'd learned from them and wanted to give him everything she was and would ever be.

Turning, he reached behind him, picked up a bouquet of red roses he'd had hidden behind the nurses' station desk. Handing her the flowers, he dropped to his knees and took her free hand in his. "Beth Taylor, this is quite possibly overboard, but after all we've been through, overboard seems the only way to go. Sso…" He paused, took a deep breath. "Will you be my girlfriend?"

Holding the flowers in one hand and the other shaking in his hand, Beth stared at Eli in confusion. "What?"

"I want you to be my girlfriend and for the whole world to know you're mine, that I want to date you and learn everything about you and spend my life with you. Say yes." He squeezed her hand gently, stroking his thumb over her skin. "Although if all that is too much but you're willing to agree to dinner, I'll take you anywhere you'd like to go."

"Eli?" Her forehead wrinkled. "What is this?"

"This is me asking you to be mine in front of our friends and coworkers."

Beth glanced around, caught Emily's eye and her friend gave her a thumbs-up signal. Nurse Rogers was smiling as if she'd played cupid and Beth and Eli had been recipients of her arrow. Even Cassidy was smiling and nodding her approval.

"Seriously, I didn't expect quite this quick a response to my text."

This time it was Eli who looked confused. On cue, she heard the resounding buzz of his phone receiving a message. Her message. Beth laughed.

He hadn't gotten her text. Not yet. He'd come for her anyway.

Of course he'd come for her anyway.

Even if he had gotten her text prior to her stepping into the hallway, he'd obviously already had this planned. Obviously had missed her as much as she had missed him and had come to set their relationship right.

Tears welled in her eyes and she squeezed his hand. "I love you, Eli. I really, really love you."

His breath caught then he grinned. "I was looking for a yes, but that'll do just fine."

He stood, took her into his arms, and kissed her until they were both breathless and the sound of clapping began to register.

Glancing around at their spectators, Beth blushed. "I wasn't expecting this." She held up the flowers. "Or you."

"I'm like a bad penny, I'm always going to turn up wherever you are."

"More like my lucky penny." She smiled at him, feeling happier than she'd have believed possible just minutes before. "And I hope so, because I need you, Eli."

"The feeling is mutual, Beth." He kissed her cheek. "I've missed you."

"Okay, you two, enough mush is enough mush," Nurse Rogers interrupted. "Beth, it's slowed down and several of the night shift crew have already arrived. Why don't you go ahead, give report and clock out?"

"Thank you," Beth said, hugged Emily, who reminded her not to say or do anything she wouldn't do, and even got surprising congratulations from Cassidy.

Beth gave report, clocked out, then turned back to Eli, realized what he was about to do and grabbed for his phone. "No. Give me that."

But he'd already seen. First shock registered on his face then a smile.

"'Night, folks," was all he said, as he slipped his phone into his pocket, reached for Beth's hand and led her out of the ICU.

The minute they were alone in the elevator, he took the phone out of his pocket and waved it in front of her. "Wow."

She shrugged. "Don't ever say I'm not a girl who doesn't give her guy what he asks for." Her lips twitched. "Just maybe not always in the time frame he wants. Sometimes I'm a little slow to trust, but I do trust you, Eli. More than I ever dreamt I could trust another person."

He hugged her to him, lifting her off her feet and spinning her around the elevator. "For the record, I'm going to ask for a lot, Beth. All your love, all your trust, all you have to give. I want it all."

She arched a brow in question, liking how he'd taken her into his arms and held her close.

"I'm going to ask for you to be mine forever."

Her breath catching, she smiled.

His chest rumbling against hers, he laughed. "You are, you know."

"I know." She hugged him close, barely able to comprehend the enormity of what they were saying. "I'm going to ask for all those things from you, too, you know?"

"They're already yours, Beth. All that I am belongs to you."

Just as she'd typed "YOURS" in all capital letters beneath the photo she'd sent him, she was his, now and forever.

Just as she knew he was hers, now and forever.

* * * * *